DEAD TROUBLE

DEAD TROUBLE

by

Jake Douglas

Dales Large Print Books
Long Preston, North Yorkshire,
BD23 4ND, England.

British Library Cataloguing in Publication Data.

Douglas, Jake
    Dead trouble.

    A catalogue record of this book is
    available from the British Library

    ISBN   1-84262-438-5 pbk

First published in Great Britain 2005 by Robert Hale Limited

Copyright © Jake Douglas 2005

Cover illustration © Faba by arrangement with
Norma Editorial S.A.

Published in Large Print 2006 by arrangement with
Robert Hale Ltd.

Dales Large Print is an imprint of Library Magna Books Ltd.

Printed and bound in Great Britain by
T.J. (International) Ltd., Cornwall, PL28 8RW

CHAPTER 1

LAST GUNFIGHT

When he rode into the town calling itself
Red Creek Flats, Deke Cutler had no
notion that the coming gunfight would be
his last as a Texas Ranger.

There was no doubt this deal would end in
gunplay and someone taking up residence
in Boot Hill. All he had to do was make sure
it wasn't him. Ten years ago he would have
been *damn certain sure* with the arrogance
and confidence of youth. Now, a couple of
years past his mid-thirties, he had to think a
little, convince himself he would walk away
from this.

He'd damn well better, because he had big
plans for the future and he was looking
forward to seeing Durango Spain again, this
time as a partner in the ranch at Red River
which Spain was working until Cutler's
retirement came due.

A different kind of retirement could be
awaiting him in this shack town – McKittrick

7

was bound to have a slew of friends handy and all he had to do was yell *Ranger!* and every hardcase within earshot would reach for his gun.

Ah, the hell with it! This was his job and it had to be done – so damn well get on with it!

It was still cool for mid-September in Red Flats, as most folk called it, dropping the 'Creek' because it was little more than a trickle and a man could step across it easily. Cutler pulled the hip-length jacket across his chest but left the lower buttons undone. The flap covered the butt of his six-gun but left a good portion of the tied-down holster exposed. Anyone who knew what to look for could see this man who forked the trail-stained sorrel down Main through the hazy dusk was a man who liked to get his gun out fast, and so he was one to be leery of.

He didn't move his head side to side, but he swivelled his eyes as the horse plodded on and he saw some men pause and squint through the fading light, all tensed-up. Others stopped dead in their tracks and made no secret of their curiosity. A stranger arriving this close to sundown was bound to arouse suspicion amongst men like these.

Two dropped their hands instinctively to

their gun butts, but, on taking a second look at Cutler, decided to leave the weapons in leather. But both hurried across the street towards the murky lights of the town's only saloon.

Cutler saw the LIVERY sign – weak, dripping tar slapped across a weathered, splintered plank and propped up against a leaky rain butt – and turned the horse through the sagging gate and on into the draughty building. Planks were warped, some missing. He wouldn't bet how rain-proof the roof was, either. But the hostler was a smiling, bright young *hombre* in bib-and-brace coveralls, one strap caught with a rusty safety pin.

'Just made it, friend – I close up at sundown.'

Cutler dismounted stiffly, half a head taller than the gangling livery man, thumbed back his dusty, sweat-dark hat.

'Business must be good,' he opined, although the broken down stalls only housed less than a dozen horses.

'Huh? Aw, you mean closin' early. Heck, I could stay open all night, but I'd have to sleep here.' The hostler winked, a big, raw-boned country kid, still with marks of fading freckles and tousled hair under a shapeless felt hat. 'Ain't been married but a couple months. Where would you rather spend your nights?'

He laughed and Cutler nodded, slapping a hand on his saddle.

'Hang that up on a peg, rub down the horse and give him some hay and a handful of oats. No more'n a handful. All right?'

'Sure. I know hosses, mister. Used to wrangle for a rodeo show.'

Sliding his rifle out of the saddle scabbard, Cutler turned his head, frowning.

'How the hell did you end up here?'

'Wife's family din' bless the marriage, you might say. Had to find someplace they wasn't likely to look.'

'Friend, you don't want to be so open, telling everyone your business. How you know her family didn't send me? Pay me to look for you...?'

The youngster blinked, then the colour faded from his face. His mouth worked but no intelligible sound escaped. He started to back off from Cutler as the rifle came out of leather and swung around in the hostler's direction.

'Listen, I...'

His hands were raised, palms out, as if he would push away the sudden menace. But Cutler shook his head.

'Relax, son. I'm not after you. Just giving you a friendly warning so you'll be a little more careful.'

Breath hissed out in relief and the young man smiled again, swallowed and wiped a grimy kerchief down his sweat-glossy face.

'Aw, mister, you scared the hell outta me!'

'Sorry. Now tell me where I'll find a man named McKittrick.'

The eyes widened.

'Kel McKittrick?' Cutler nodded. 'Well, if you're one of his friends, I guess you'll find him in the back room of the saloon. Him and his pards kinda get together most nights.'

'S'posing I wasn't a "friend" of his?'

The hostler studied him closely, taking in the trail clothes and their signs of long, hard travel. The gaunt square-jawed face, the cool, searching grey-green eyes and the whip-lean stance of a man at ease holding a rifle – and the way the jacket flap had been now pushed back behind the Colt's butt, making it easier to reach.

'Er ... well then, I ... wouldn't walk right on in, mister.'

'What would you do?'

A tongue flickered across the suddenly dry lips. 'I – I dunno as how I'd care to go

11

anywheres near that place.'

'But if you did? If you had to...?'

'If I had to ... why, I reckon I'd go out through my back door.' The hostler gestured towards the shadowed rear of the big barnlike building. 'Work my way round my corrals. Got some half-broke fillies in the second one, so I'd walk wide: they sniff the man-smell and they get all frisky an' squeal and holler.'

'I'll give 'em a wide berth,' Cutler allowed.

'Well, then I'd go around the back of the dark buildin' across the lot past the corrals, cross the street where there ain't no lamplight spillin' outta doorways and go down the alley between the gen'l store and the barber's. That'd put me within six feet of the door that leads into that back room from the saloon yard. The *dark* saloon yard.'

Cutler nodded. 'Sounds like a sensible thing to do.' He reached into a pocket and flipped a silver dollar at the hostler who picked the coin out of the air dexterously. 'Be one or two more when I come back. Which might be a mite faster than I arrived. So I'll need the horse ready.'

'How about a fresh one? Got me a buckskin I been workin' on and he's full-broke to the saddle and rider now.'

'He? Stallion?'

'Geldin'. Cost you – aw – thirty-five? An' the dun there.'

Cutler asked to see the animal and liked its lines.

'Son, you ain't gonna make much money here with your prices. I'm on expenses, so I'll give you fifty with that Denver saddle throwed in. I keep the dun for a spare.'

The kid, looking pleased at the mention of fifty dollars, suddenly paled again and looked mighty worried.

'What's wrong?'

'That saddle you want belongs to Mr McKittrick.'

Cutler smiled crookedly.

'Then we got a deal. *He* won't be needing it after tonight.'

Kel McKittrick was a roughneck in his forties who had lived on the outside of the law all his brutal life. He was a mighty tough man, had been through all kinds of hardships, including near-drowning in the flooded Pecos one time when he saved himself by pulling his rescuer out of the saddle into the raging water before grabbing the horse's tail and allowing the animal to fight its way to the bank. The Good Samaritan, of course, drowned, but McKittrick never even looked back as he rode off.

He had fought Indians, from raiding parties to hand-to-hand knife combats over rights to a squaw. He had killed stage guards and drivers and even a few passengers, and if a rancher or his cowhands tried to stop him rustling their beef, they were inevitably marked for lonely graves.

Kel McKittrick had no conscience. Not once did he ever think about the people he killed or caused to be killed. They had stood between him and what he wanted so they had to be removed and the quickest and surest way was with gun or knife.

It was McKittrick's cold-bloodedness that was his undoing.

He made a habit of visiting a whore over in the nearby town of Big Hat, a slightly more salubrious place than Red Flats, and he had been quite taken with the woman, thought about moving her back to the Flats. Then one night he looked in another room of her house, in search of a drink, tequila and moonshine already scouring his belly but leaving him thirsting for more.

In a bed against a wall, was a girl, twelve years old, her chestnut hair glinting with tight curls. Her skin was porcelain-smooth,

14

soft as goosedown, silken. Her screams awakened the mother still asleep in her rumpled bed which she had been sharing with McKittrick.

She came in like a cyclone in a nightgown, wielding a length of fence paling she kept under the bed – sometimes her customers were rougher than she liked and had to be subdued. She 'subdued' McKittrick with a well-placed swing of the paling, pulled her hysterical daughter out from beneath him and told him to get out, that she'd kill him if ever he laid another finger on the girl.

When McKittrick recovered he laid more than a finger on the child – and he left the whore bleeding and battered so that she was out of business permanently. It took her a long time to get over that beating and then she went looking for the girl. And found her in an outlaw camp, being passed from man to man, plied with liquor, far gone, out of her head, never knowing what was happening to her.

The whore couldn't hope to get near McKittrick, but she went to the Rangers and told them where he hung out, how the original hideout, used by other men on the dodge, had gradually built up into the shack town of Red Flats.

The Rangers sent their top man to get McKittrick, one of the most wanted outlaws in the state.

That man was Deke Cutler, and now he was crouched in the darkness outside the weather-raw door of the Red Flats saloon, loaded rifle in hand, ready to go get his man.

He could hear muted voices through the wall, likker-roughened, only an occasional swear word coming through the door so he could understand it. He listened carefully a little longer. *Five,* he figured by the slight difference in the tones of the voices that he could just make out.

Well, he'd had better odds and likely they wouldn't change soon, so...

He drove his right boot against the door at lock-level and wood splintered. He went in shooting, dull amber light washing over the smoke-hazed room, leaving plenty of shadows. The rifle blasted and the well-oiled lever had never worked so fast and efficiently. Flame stabbed, moved slightly left and stabbed again, swung right, flared, the muzzle moving in a deadly arc.

Men threw up their arms. One man screamed. Another cussed a blue streak, down on one knee but bringing up a gun. Cutler gave him another bullet and he went over backwards, body twisted in an impossible position. A man ran for the other door and Cutler cut him down, then spun away as a bullet tore through his right forearm, chewing at the muscle, blood and flesh spraying.

The impact slammed him against the wall as the gunman stepped out of a shadowed corner. Through the red haze of pain, even as he fumbled for his six-gun, Cutler recognized McKittrick.

'So they sent the goddamn Rangers!' the killer snorted and spat, bringing up his smoking pistol. 'Well, hope they give you a good funeral, Deke!'

Cutler dropped, his Colt slippery with his blood in his right hand. He rolled across the floor as McKittrick's bullets tore into the warped boards. Then he flopped on to his back, Colt in his left hand now, and as the killer lunged at him so as to get a clear shot, Cutler fired upwards.

The bullet splintered the table which was in the way and slivers of wood flew into McKittrick's face. He clawed at his eyes and Cutler put two bullets into his belly, a third into his chest.

McKittrick was dead before he hit the floor.

Cutler worked up to his feet, feeling a little lightheaded, arm dripping blood. He was half-crouched in the middle of the room, surrounded by dead men, when he heard a faint sound behind him. He started to turn but wasn't fast enough and the bullet took him in the back, under the left shoulder, and slammed him across the table. As he slid to the floor, through the red pain and the fast-approaching oblivion, he saw the kid from the livery standing there with a smoking rifle in his hands. He smiled.

'Should've asked me my name, mister– It's McKittrick, too. Kel was my half-brother. No-good son of a bitch! Least he won't bother my wife no more. Nor anyone else. Obliged to you for killin' him for me. No one's gonna miss him... So I'll just say– *Adios.*'

The blackness had descended on Cutler before the kid stepped out into the night, whistling.

CHAPTER 2

SIX LONG MONTHS

The man with the shoulder-length hair sitting at the table in the corner of the bar room spluttered into his beer and half-choked. He coughed and spat and wiped at his mouth and streaming eyes with a kerchief, clearing his throat as he glared at the kid standing by his table.

'*What?*' he croaked. 'He was *what?*'

'A Ranger,' repeated Kid McKittrick, still flushed with excitement from what he had pulled off in the room out back of the saloon. 'A goddamn Texas Ranger, Long!'

Everyone had heard the shooting but no one had gone to investigate. Red Flats was that kind of town. It was healthier that way for all concerned.

'Suspected him right off. When he left to go after Kel, I went through his saddlebags, found a badge pinned to the inside of the flap. Figured it was best to kill him.'

The long-haired man stood slowly, his

19

small eyes mere glinting dark dots in his face now as the lids pinched down. He was aware that the other drinkers were watching – and listening. He spoke to them without taking his gaze from the kid who showed signs of unease now, hands sweaty against the rifle he still held.

'You know what this crazy bastard has done?' the long-haired man asked the room and, not waiting for an answer, added, 'He's gone and back-shot a Texas goddamn *Ranger!*'

If McKittrick expected applause and congratulations, he was mighty disappointed. There was a stunned silence at first, then cusses from every corner of the crowded room, then shouts and a few fists were shaken. McKittrick swallowed, turning to face the men who were yelling at him.

'Damn fool kid!'

'Chris'sakes, we'll have a whole blame troop comin' in here lookin' for him!'

'Jesus, kid, din' no one tell you you *never* kill a Ranger!'

'Might's well put a gun to your own head!'

Flushed and his heart hammering, McKittrick yelled,

'I never killed him! He's dyin', I guess, but...'

That seemed to make matters worse. The kid looked to Longhair for some sort of guidance. 'He come lookin' for Kel – you know what hell Kel an' his pards've put us all through lately.' He stopped to clear his throat. 'I for one was fed up with all the beatin's and kickin's I was gettin' an' the way he was playin' round with my wife. No one seemed game to go up agin him, so I figured let that big sonuver who rode in take care of him – then I shot him, too.'

'You made one big mistake, kid,' Longhair said quietly.

McKittrick was sweating, saw there was no help here from anyone. Instead of being looked on as some kind of hero, they seemed ready to kill him. He brought up the rifle, lever clashing, and started to back towards the door, eyes wild.

'You try to stop me an' I'll shoot! I *will*.'

No one tried to stop him: the sooner he was out of town the better.

They heard him go not five minutes later, forking the sleek buckskin he had prepared for the Ranger, his wife trailing him on a slower dun, skirts and hair flying.

'What the hell we gonna do?' a man asked Longhair. 'We'll have to get rid of that Ranger. Someone'll come lookin' for him.'

21

Longhair pointed to a man who was obviously the worse for drink slouched in a corner. He was middle-aged, unshaven, dressed in soiled frock-coat and grey-flannel trousers that had seen better times.

'Throw a bucket of water over him and drag him out to look at the Ranger. Kid said he ain't quite dead yet.'

'Hey! The hell you got in mind!'

Longhair's eyes were tight and small again. 'Like you said, Blackie, they'll come lookin'. That we don't want.' He jerked a thumb to the drunk in the chair. 'He used to be a sawbones – killed some kid on the operatin' table back East an' crawled into a likker bottle and been livin' there ever since–'

'Christ! He couldn't do nothin'. Anyway, what the hell you want him to do?'

'He can tell us if the Ranger can travel. If he can, we take him down to Big Hat and dump him at the infirmary there. Better if the Rangers find him alive or bein' looked after than dead. We all swear he never come here. They might still come but it won't be the same, like if they're lookin' for someone who killed one of their kind, but we can tell 'em it was Kid McKittrick shot him if we have to, give 'em a trail to follow, get 'em away from here.'

The men looked dubious.

'Risky, Long,' said Blackie.

'Sure. But better'n havin' to close down the whole blame town and clear out – or have it done by Rangers out for blood! It's our only chance, way I see it. Now get that old has-been sobered-up as much as you can and get him on his feet. Chuck, Mungo, you come with me and we'll see what we can do for the Ranger till Doc has a look at him.'

They thought he was mad. But now that McKittrick was dead, Longhair was the most feared man in Red Flats. They moved to obey.

The drunken ex-sawbones let out a strangled, choking yell as someone tipped a pail of cold water over him. Someone else hauled him out of his chair and slapped his face until his eyes began to focus. Then they shook him, took him out to the horse-trough, dunked him half a dozen times, and dragged him out to the room where five dead men and one dying awaited him.

They found Longhair and Mungo crouched over Deke Cutler.

'How's he doin', Long?' asked Blackie, holding one arm of the sagging, drenched doctor who was swaying from side to side, wondering what was happening to him.

'Don't think he's gonna make it,' Longhair said grimly. 'Slap that sawbones around until he knows where he's at. *Do* it, goddamnit! If this son of a bitch dies we're all in more trouble'n you can shake a stick at!'

Blackie's hand smacked back and forth across the doctor's slack face. He moaned and protested feebly but didn't seem any more aware than previously.

'Ahhh! It ain't no good, Long! He ain't gonna help. You ask me, we better bury the Ranger and quit the Flats before a troop comes ridin' in and kicks us out! We're finished here!'

Doctor Hugo Farraday was a burly man who wheezed a lot. His fingers were stained darkly with nicotine, as was the bushy moustache under his large nose. Anyone coming out of chloroform and seeing that face looking down at them could be forgiven for thinking they had ended up in Hell.

But when he spoke, his voice was soothing, quiet, gentle – as were his big hands.

'Deke? That right, they call you "Deke"?'

Cutler's heavy-lidded eyes fluttered a little and he was some time before he nodded. He tried to talk but his voice was too raspy for anything to be understood. Doc Farraday's right hand pressed him gently back against the bedsheets.

'Try to relax. Just wanted to make sure you were coming out of the anaesthetic. It'll be some time yet before you can speak or do anything much except lie there and moan and groan.' He smiled, the yellowed moustache masking much of the smile. 'My name's Doctor Farraday. They brought you in from Red Flats. Someone shot you in the back and you've taken a bullet in your right arm which has made quite a mess of all the things that go to work it smoothly. I've done what I can and you're too weak to be moved anyplace that can do better, so I'm afraid you're between that legendary rock and a hard place. Are you understanding any of this?'

The eyes fluttered partly open again. There was a faint gargling sound and then the slightest movement of the head: a nod.

'You are a very tough man, friend,' Farraday said with undisguised admiration in his voice. 'How you survived the ride from Red Flats hanging over a horse, I'll never know. But I have to tell you, Deke, that's it's going to be a long, long time before you get on a horse in any manner. Your left lung has been nicked, splinters of bone have been driven into your muscles. It's going to hurt like red-hot hell once you try to move things around. But that won't be yet awhile. Not trying to depress you. I just believe that patients should know their condition and what may or may not happen to them.'

Deke Cutler continued to look up through slitted eyelids. His left arm was strapped across his chest. His right was heavily bandaged from wrist to bicep. He managed to lift one finger of his right hand, the index one, and he scratched at the sheet several times.

Farraday frowned.

'You want something?' A slight sideways movement of the head. *Scratch, scratch, scratch!* 'Er ... you want to *know* something? Want me to tell you...'

A nod.

'I – see. Now what do you wish to know? Of course! How long before you are better? Am I right?'

Another slight nod and an obvious straining to open the eye further, a quickening of the breathing. Farraday reached down and gently squeezed his right hand.

'I can't tell, Deke. By rights you should be dead. Whatever you did before – cowhand, stage driver, or whatever – well, I doubt you'll be fit for even light work under six months.'

Deke Cutler's big body went rigid under the sheet covering him. There was a deep frown, the head moved back and forth. Farraday made gentling sounds, leaning over him, drawing the sheet up to his chin.

'Don't you worry about it – I'll pull you through, with your help. Just accept that it may – *will* – be quite a long time and that you might have to think about some new kind of work. It will be easier in the long run if you do that.'

Deke Cutler's mind was still too fuzzy and dizzy from the chloroform and he couldn't have put the words together if he wanted to.

But something deep down told him clearly that he *would* pull through and he would go back to Rangering – *even if it killed him!*

Even though still only semi-conscious, he felt like laughing at this last. *Even if it killed him!*

Christ! His life was already hanging by a thread.

Mrs Farraday, a plumpish woman with silver streaks in her hair and a smiling face, opened the door to the big, dusty man who wore the circled-star Texas Ranger badge on his vest.

Her smile warmed.

'Well, you look as if a cup of coffee and some of my biscuits wouldn't go amiss. Come you in.'

The big man smiled, hat in hand now, sweat-tousled black hair pasted to his high forehead. He murmured, 'Thank you, ma'am' as he shuffled into the room. She led him through to the kitchen and proceeded to get him some vittles. He apologized for his appearance.

'Ridden out from San Angelo, ma'am. My, that coffee sure smells good. Ma'am, I b'lieve your husband has a patient here named Deke Cutler? I'm Ranger Dal Beattie, by the way.'

'Pleased to meet you, I'm sure. Yes, we have Mr Cutler here.' Her smile had faded now. 'Very poorly, I'm afraid. Fever has him in its grip and Doctor Farraday is afraid the infection will turn to pneumonia.'

Beattie frowned. 'We heard he was bad hit – but he's been here a month or so now, ain't that right?'

'Yes. But the doctor will explain. You eat up and I'll fetch him.'

Doc Farraday shook hands briefly with

Beattie as his wife poured him a cup of coffee and left the room. He told the Ranger about Cutler's wounds.

'By rights, ought to be dead. 'Bout the toughest man I've ever seen and I used to work the Cherry Creek goldfields in Colorado.'

'He is gonna make it though, Doc?'

Farraday obviously didn't want to commit himself and the Ranger grew impatient as he hedged.

'All right. What happened to him?'

'Brought in by some of the men from Red Flats. They were very eager to stress that they found him lying beside the trail from Big Hat here to their town, but I rather think Deke Cutler was ... injured in Red Flats.'

Dal Beattie's mouth was taut now as he accepted a fresh cup of coffee from the doctor.

'Red Flats. We been lookin' at that dump for a long time. Deke must've gotten a lead. He was after Kel McKittrick...' He stood abruptly. 'I reckon it's time we closed down that damn outlaw nest.'

'I am surprised it hasn't been done before, Ranger.' There was censure in the medic's voice.

'Well, Doc, it suited us to know of a place where outlaws gathered. We could keep an eye on 'em, but it's been gettin' too damn big lately. There a telegraph office in town?'

Farraday told him how to get to it, wondered why Beattie hadn't asked to see Cutler. The Ranger merely said he didn't want to disturb him.

He sent off his wire and by noon the eight Rangers who had been waiting at the Butterfield way station on Mad Dog Mesa drifted into Big Hat one by one during the course of the afternoon, a couple arriving after dusk.

By midnight they were in position around Red Flats, and by sun-up the first fires were started.

The heavily armed Rangers waited in their hiding places. They didn't have to wait long before the raw-eyed men below, nursing rotgut hangovers, began coming out of the trash-built shanties and lean-tos. The smoke made them cough and when they saw how many fires were burning – ten in all – it even penetrated their hangovers that this day brought big trouble, About the same time, the Rangers opened up, shooting to kill, aiming to put Red Flats off the map for ever. The outlaws fell and scattered, running for horses, but found the livery almost totally consumed by now, the horses having been driven out and up the slope to spread out amongst the timber.

They could only turn and flee.

It was brief and bloody – and complete. Two Rangers went down, one never to rise again, the other with a leg wound. Longhair seemed to survive right to the end and finally it was he and Dal Beattie who confronted each other behind the charred and still-blazing ruins of the saloon.

Longhair was bleeding from two minor bullet wounds, one a scalp crease, and his face was streaked with blood as the big Ranger stepped out from behind a charred, sagging door.

'Been a long time since Fort Kelso, Long, you son of a bitch!'

'Not long enough for you, Beattie!' Longhair triggered his shotgun and Beattie jumped back behind the door. But buckshot chewed a large hunk out of the woodwork and some of the balls took him in the neck and upper body. He stepped out, working lever and trigger on his rifle with the butt jammed against his hip.

Longhair reeled, trying to reload, snapped the Greener closed too soon, jamming the cartridge. Three slugs stitched across his chest and he went down. Beattie took a step forward and became aware that he was soaked with his own blood. He put up a hand and felt the wounds in his neck. One had torn some kind of artery and he knew he wasn't going to make it. He'd just had his last gunfight and there was nothing he could do about it – except lie down and die.

But Red Flats and its inhabitants was no more.

Deke Cutler eased to his feet from the chair Farraday had placed for him under the red elm-tree not far from the house. He reached for his stick and wavered a little as he walked back towards the house, taking short, slow steps.

Mrs Farraday was hanging some washing on the line.

'You're looking better today, Deke.'

He was gaunt and pale, face knobbly with high cheekbones and hard-cut jawline. His eyes were sunken, smeared darkly underneath. But he managed a small smile for the doctor's wife.

'Ought to be – getting better – ma'am.' He was still very short of breath. 'Over two months now....'

'Slow and easy, Doctor Farraday says, and he's right, Deke. Don't get impatient. Just follow orders.'

He nodded and although he would never admit it, he was mighty glad to flop on to his bed in a small room behind the infirmary and stretch out.

When the hell am I going to get on my feet properly? he asked himself, then held up his right arm, trying to flex the fingers but they barely moved.

Goddamn! And this was my gunarm!

After the third month, and some visits from fellow Rangers who could find the time to come see him, Cutler confided in Farraday that he was afraid he would never be able to use his right arm in a gunfight again.

'The forearm muscle and nerves have been badly mangled, Deke. There isn't a lot I can do.'

'That means there is *something*, doc. I want to try it, no matter how little – or crazy.'

Farraday studied him, knew here was a man who had lived by the gun for many years – and likely wouldn't survive if he couldn't use a firearm again. Anyway, he had brought the Ranger back from the dead, so it was up to him to equip him as well as possible for what might lay ahead.

It hurt.

Strengthening the fingers wasn't so bad – plunging them endlessly into a bowl of rice-grains; later, graduating to loosely-packed sand. That was when it began to hurt – the rough sand, peppered with gravel, tore at the flesh around his nails, got underneath the nails, caused tenderness. But Farraday made him keep on and soon the fingertips and the knuckles became calloused and there was more flexibility in the fingers themselves. Impatient, Deke strapped on his six-gun and tried to draw. He fumbled badly, dropped the gun over and over. Farrady was angry.

'You damn fool! You're not ready. Trying too soon and failing only makes it worse, brings on depression!'

Chastened, Cutler returned to plunging his hand into the sand, hour after hour, day after day. At night he sat squeezing a rubber ball. And then Farraday brought in a friend he said would work on the damaged forearm.

The 'friend' was Indian, an old man with white hair under a battered beaverskin hat and smelly animal totems woven into his long braids. His hands looked deformed to Cutler, knuckles bulging arthritically, fingers twisted.

But when he went to work on Deke's arm, manipulating, massaging, twisting painfully, even tying the whole forearm in greenhide strips, then wetting them so that they contracted excruciatingly, like a vice, Cutler, miraculously, began to feel the strength returning to the arm. It would never be the same as before but it was improving.

First, he could shoot his rifle pretty near as well as before and he knew he would improve with practice. Using a six-gun was more difficult and the old Indian almost pulled his trigger finger from its socket, twisting and making the joints grate, before the suppleness returned. His wrist was also manhandled painfully – but effectively.

Cutler knew he would never be able to draw and shoot like the 'half-brother to lightning' as legend had styled him. Something was gone from his gun arm and would never return. But the old Indian's equanimity and natural composure made him persevere and one day, when he was hitting the target post consistently and he could run the length of the trail up the slope to the dead ruins of Red Flats without undue distress, he announced to the doctor:

'Doc, I'm ready to go back to the Rangers.'

Farraday looked startled, as if he had forgotten his goal of preparing Deke to return to his old way of life. The Indian lifted a finger up beside his left temple and said in his whispering voice:

'Go well, and with care, Ironheart.'

Six months and eight days after being shot in the back by Kid McKittrick, Deke Cutler rode out of Big Hat, ready to go a-Rangering again.

CHAPTER 3

RED RIVER

Durango Spain was a man who had just turned fifty. His wife, Karen, was just over twenty years his junior.

He was a beefy, ruggedly handsome man, running to a little fat now, although he worked his butt off on the Red River ranch that he was buying with partner Deke Cutler. The closest town was Wichita Falls and the spread was only a frog's leap across the river from the Indian Territory, out of bounds to all state lawmen. It needed a federal warrant or marshal legally to go after a man within the Territory's boundaries. Which was why so many men riding outside the law made the Territory their home: *Badman's Territory* most folk along the Red called it.

Spain was building some holding-corrals in a high canyon north-west of the ranch with a few of the cowhands when Jimmy Taggart came riding in, looking flushed. He jumped from his horse before it had skidded to a halt and stumbled as he floundered his way to where Spain and Hal Tripp were setting up a top rail between two posts.

'The hell's your hurry, Jimmy?' Spain said as the youngster dusted off his hands and came hurrying forward.

'Hell, look at him, Durango!' said Tripp with a laugh. 'I swear he's wet his pants with excitement an' don't want us to see!'

Jimmy paused, getting his breath under control, standing tall now so they could see his trousers' front was dry. He scowled at the grinning Tripp, turned to Spain.

'Someone to see you down at the house, Durango,' Taggart panted.

Spain frowned – with maybe an involuntary tightening of his stomach muscles.

'Yeah? Who the hell's rid all the way out here to see me?'

'He ain't just come from town, he's come up from San Antone, he says.'

Spain tensed even more.

'Well, you gonna tell me who it is or stand there being smart-mouth?'

Jimmy looked slightly hurt at his boss's tone. 'Well,' he said, 'it's Deke Cutler. That feller you said was your sidekick when you was a Ranger.'

Spain was stiff as the oak post he and Hal Tripp had been manhandling now.

'Deke? You sure?'

'That's who he said he was. Seemed to know Mrs Spain. Was her sent me to get you. "Pronto", she said, and she don't usually use words like that.'

Hal Tripp was sober now, watching Durango Spain.

'Thought Cutler was dead,' Tripp said carefully.

'That's what I heard,' Spain said slowly. 'Backshot by some kid down in Red Flats, wherever the hell that is. Thought it was odd. Deke was never one to turn his back on anyone likely to shoot him.' He dropped the chisel he had been using and hooked the hammer over an upright post, slapping his leather work-gloves together, dust flying. 'Well, I'd best get on down and see this here living ghost.'

'Looks like he's been poorly for a spell,' volunteered Jimmy Taggart. 'Walks kinda slow and keeps rubbin' at his right arm, like it hurts. Kind of catches his breath every so often. But he looks mighty dangerous.'

Spain smiled crookedly.

'Sure sounds like Deke.'

And when he rode in half an hour later and saw the man sitting on the porch, nursing a cup of coffee, Durango knew his old sidekick was truly alive and kicking. Cutler stood, grinning as he extended his right hand.

Durango tried to seem pleased to see Deke, said all the right words, but there was a stiffness about his manner that Deke couldn't help but notice.

After a little good-natured badgering Spain sat down beside Cutler and Karen brought a tray of fresh coffee and biscuits. She was a small woman, no more than five-two, three, maybe, wheat-coloured hair piled up to make her look a little taller. Her eyes were clear blue and steady, focusing on the face of whomever she was talking to. She wore a plain grey dress, pinched in at the waist, showing a good figure, and she moved easily.

'I couldn't believe it when I saw him riding in,' she told her husband, but looking at Cutler now. 'Not after the news we'd had three or four months ago.'

'Three or four months ago I *was* more dead than alive,' Cutler said, taking another cup of coffee.

'It's true then?' Spain asked. 'Some kid backshot you, Deke?'

40

Cutler sipped his coffee and nodded soberly.

'Kil McKittrick's kid brother.'

'Never knew he had one.'

'Wish I'd known.' Cutler briefly told about the gunfight with Kel McKittrick and his men. 'The Kid and his wife are both dead. *Bandidos* took 'em at Sabinas. As for me, some old drunk living with the outlaws patched me up enough for them to take me into Big Hat and a proper doctor. They didn't want my body found in Red Flats.' He coughed for a minute, hand covering his mouth. 'Sorry. Lung still catches me now and again. Was a damn long six months pulling through, Durango. Then the Rangers told me they didn't want me.'

Spain looked at him sharply.

'They must be loco!'

Cutler shook his head.

'Dunno about that. But the troop medic wouldn't pass me for active duty. Said I'd have to take a desk job for six months and then they'd review "my situation".'

'Oh, Deke, that's terrible,' Karen sympathized. 'After all the years you gave them! The men you brought to justice!'

Spain was watching him carefully.

'I know you, you didn't take any desk job,'

he said slowly.

'Not me. I quit.'

'You quit! Man, you only had a few months to go to qualify for a pension. Ten full years of service!' When Cutler said nothing, Spain added, quietly: 'I was sort of counting on you to help out here, with your pension, Deke. When we thought you was alive, I mean.'

'Sorry, Durango, but there's no pension,' Cutler told him gently. 'New rules, now. They only pay for one month's doctoring if a Ranger's wounded in line of duty.'

'But that's – it's *unfair!*' said Karen with feeling.

'Pinching pennies, Karen. Politicians now have a say in how the Rangers are run. So much money's set aside for 'em to operate on and they have to account for every cent to the State Senate. Everyone's swamped in paperwork. Thing is, it means Doc Farraday, feller who nursed me through, is out of pocket. I sent him what I had but there's more owing...'

Spain frowned.

'You mean – you're coming here nigh on a year before we figured on, and not bringing any money for the ranch? In fact, you *owe* money!'

'Durango! Please!'

But Spain ignored his wife, hard grey gaze on his old sidekick.

Cutler met and held the stare.

'That's about the size of it, Durango,' Deke said flatly. 'I'm happy to pay Doc Farraday out of my share of the profits. That'd be OK, wouldn't it?'

'Of course Deke ... Durango just means we're – surprised, *and* pleased, of course, to see you, but–'

'But the spread ain't doing all that good,' cut in Spain.

'Your last letter said–'

'My last letter, Deke, was writ months ago, and since then I was told you were dead. No, the ranch is fighting it hard, *amigo* – near-drought, Indians, occasional raids by fellers cutting across from the Territory.'

Karen was frowning at her husband but he turned a little so he didn't have to look at her. Cutler frowned, too.

'There's talk of a big Indian uprising,' Spain said slowly. 'Comanches are s'posed to be behind it... Territory's also called "The Indian Nations", you know. Or just "The Nations".'

'Yeah. Seems I arrived at the wrong time...'

'Aaah – hell! You're here now and this kinda living will help you recover completely and with what both of us know about ranching – we'll have the profits up in no time.'

'Then there are *some* profits now?'

'Sure. Pretty damn few, but I guess we don't need to buy a bottle of red ink just yet.' He sounded reluctant to admit things weren't all that bad when you got right down to it. They were *difficult* but – manageable. For now, leastways.

Karen lifted to her toes and kissed Cutler on the cheek.

'It'll be so good to have you with us, Deke!'

He grinned.

'You dunno how good it feels to be here.'

'Well, let's go have a drink to celebrate, huh?' Spain said and the others followed him into the coolness of the ranch house.

Deke wondered why he felt heavy with disappointment. He had expected to feel way happier than this on his arrival. Maybe it was Durango's cool 'welcome.'...

Although he hated every minute of it, Deke Cutler spent the first few days mooching around the ranch house or walking quietly down by the river. He mounted his horse daily, rode it around the yard and out to the nearest pasture, doing things easy; that long ride up from San Antone had taken a lot out of him and he needed time to recover.

There weren't a lot of cattle but what there were showed the effects of poor graze in lack of weight, bony bodies and dull coats. The grass was brown and browsed way down to stubble. Durango had men up in the high meadows cutting hay and this was transported down to the main pastures and distributed from buckboards. A costly method.

The river still flowed well enough but the water level was down and ribbons of cracked mud showed on each bank. Beyond to the north was the Indian Territory and he could see green trees and slopes of high, waving grass.

He suggested to Spain that they send a team over to bring down some of that more succulent fodder.

Durango looked at him, thumbing back his hat.

'I send six men, I'll be lucky to get three back – and they're likely to be toting gunshot wounds.'

Deke frowned, stiffening.

'The outlaws are that close? Thought they

holed up deeper in the hills, amongst all those hidden canyons and valleys?'

'Most of 'em do, I guess, but there're some keep an eye on the river spreads, see what they can lift, sell cheap to Kansas – Sunflower State my foot! Claim they don't like longhorns because they carry tick fever but them Kansans'll buy Texas beef if they can get it cheap from the rustlers.'

'That why the spread's not doing so good? Rustlers?'

Durango nodded.

'Back-shooting bastards. Can't risk sending our men over there when they're a cinch to get shot at – maybe killed, Deke.'

'You got men riding patrol over here, don't you?'

Spain exhibited a trace of exasperation but made it disappear almost as soon as it showed.

'When I can spare 'em. I keep telling you, we're working tight here, Deke.'

Cutler's stare was level and questioning. 'Still – surely we can protect our herds!'

'Look, Deke. We both worked spreads before we met in the Rangers. I rode with the early trail herds as well and we agreed that I had the most experience with cows. So, I found this place – my ten years were up just over a year ago now. I got my pittance of a pension after dodging lead and arrows and Christ knows what else for the goddamn Rangers. You put in what money you had and we put down a deposit on this place, aiming to pay off the rest from the profits.' He paused to stare back coldly at Deke. 'And the profits just ain't all that good. That's the plain truth, Deke.'

Cutler thought for a moment.

'You're not telling me that ... we're behind in the bank repayments?'

Spain nodded.

'A ways. Not too bad. But every spread along the river has fallen behind because of the drought. We ain't alone.'

'I don't care how much company we've got, we shouldn't be behind at all! I sent you half my pay regular.'

'And damn glad of every cent – till it stopped after you were shot and we thought you were dead.' Spain sighed. 'That's it, Deke. Bringing in feed for the cows, setting up that windmill you see ... all takes dollars.'

Cutler started to speak but held back. He had seen the new-looking piano in the parlour – he knew Karen played a little. There were the Eastern rugs covering half the parlour floor. A damn good dining-table with upholstered chairs with what Karen had told him were 'spade' backs. He had seen furniture stores in the bigger towns and cities, some of the Gulf ports, and he'd seen overstuffed sofas and matching chairs like Spain had, and rolltop desks, too, and knew they cost plenty – especially if they had to be shipped out here with enough care to avoid damage. And there was glass in all the windows – practically unheard of on the frontier – which were trimmed with good quality curtains...

He didn't grudge Karen some comfort: hell, most frontier marriages foundered because of lack of everyday comfort, but when repayments of the bank loan were falling behind...

'We better go over the books when you have time, Durango.'

Spain didn't like that. His face looked very handsome and strong, but it was plain he was riled.

'Maybe Karen can show me if you're too busy,' Deke suggested.

'We'll sort something out,' Spain told him gruffly. 'Look, Deke, I've worked a butt and a half off keeping this place running, looking forward to your arrival – with your pension or without. Too bad it's without, but we'll figure something. But what I'm saying is: I been out here a long time now, watching Karen do without all the things she was used to before she married me, and I know the river now and how things are here – it's no good you riding in figuring to be a new broom and start sweeping out things you don't like or understand. Just leave it be a spell longer and we'll be squared away with the bank – and everyone else.'

Everyone else! Judas, Cutler wondered, who the hell *else* do we owe!

At least it would give him something to think about until he was strong enough to add some real weight to running this place.

Maybe the name they had chosen for the spread was just a little too appropriate.

The *Shoestring* spread...

He was feeling pretty good one bright morning ten days later, where the sun blazed in a cloudless blue sky, and he figured to ride out along the river and look at the boundaries.

He was forking a grey these days, a good strong horse, with an easy-going nature, but packed with muscle and knowing when to use it without waiting for the urging of rowelling spurs. He had his rifle and his six-gun. He hadn't yet done any practice with

49

this latter. He felt kind of ashamed to admit to Spain that he had lost a good deal of his old gun speed and accuracy. But the guns were a comfort to him and he watched the country across the Red River, looking for shadows that would tell him some of the men who rode the Territory were keeping an eye on him.

He thought he saw riders topping-out on a rise but the trees were moving too much with a strong breeze over there to allow him a clear view. Could be Indians – Spain had warned they were often hostile lately. He would need to stay alert. After he'd watered the grey at the river and then ridden back south-east, following the bank, he stopped suddenly, sliding the rifle clear of leather. Deke listened, patting the horse's neck to keep it still and quiet. *Yeah!* He had heard right – a human voice, calling something, then running footsteps and a sudden snarling and squealing that set the hairs standing on the back of his neck.

He slipped out of the saddle, leaving the grey with trailing reins, crouched a little and made his way up the slope, gasping some at a sharp pain in the lung that had been nicked by Kid McKittrick's bullet.

The squealing was high-pitched now,

followed by snuffling snarls and, heart pounding, still crouching, he went down full length, using the rifle barrel to part the bushes in front of him. Cutler stiffened, felt his eyes fly wide in surprise.

Below him in a draw where water had lain long enough to make a mire and a slushy pool, a huge man stripped to the waist was knee-deep in mud, lunging at a trapped and bleeding wild boar with a ... Deke wasn't sure what it was. At first he thought it was a sword, then he saw that it had a long-bladed spearhead, about fifteen inches of blued steel on a short handle no more than two feet in length.

The man was jabbing at the boar that had several wounds in its hide. The curving tusks slashed at the tormentor and the man leapt back, swearing in some language Cutler didn't recognize. Wounded and likely dying, the boar made a last desperate attempt to escape past the prodding spear. Mud flew in a fanning spray and water geysered as the huge animal lunged through the mud and slush, the lowered head forcing a brown bow wave as the raking tusks sought the big man.

He leapt clear of the slush, let out a roar and while still airborne, took the slippery

51

handle of the spear in both hands and drove the glinting blade down between the boar's heaving shoulders. The snarling squeal of pain hurt Deke's ears and the animal lunged and bucked in its final spasms, blood gushing from its mouth, as the man leaned all his weight on the spear, driving it completely through the hairy body and pinning the boar to the ground.

Deke hadn't been conscious of holding a breath but now he let it out slowly, hissing between his teeth. He had never seen anything like it, not even when Indians, a dozen at a time, cornered a bear and ran it through with stone-headed lances while others shot arrow after arrow into the hairy body.

But this had been man against beast, one on one.

The big man below tossed his head, long muddy hair flying up out of his eyes as he lifted his face skywards and let out a great roar of triumph, brandishing the bloody spear.

Cutler began to slide back but suddenly froze as something cold and very sharp sliced through the loose folds of his shirt and pricked his skin. He felt a thread of warm blood crawl across his flesh as he turned his head slowly.

He thought he had had his share of shocks for the day but here was another one.

A totally bald black man, slim and tall as a tree, he seemed from Cutler's angle, and wearing some sort of red robe over one shoulder, belted about the middle, stood over him, prodding him with a long, slim-handled spear which had an oval metal blade about six inches long, now only a hair's breadth from his flesh.

'Stay!' the man said in a deep voice and even that single word seemed to have a lilt of music in it.

Deke Cutler stayed put. He had never seen a man like this before – and he had never seen a spear like the man held ready to drive deep into his body if he so much as twitched a finger.

CHAPTER 4

SPEARMAN

Cutler didn't move. The black man, well over six feet tall, and his spear an extra six inches above that, didn't move, either. He called out to the mud-and-blood-spattered spearman below in a sing-song language. The big white man looked up sharply, wiping mud and grit from the wooden handle of his strange weapon and then started up the slope.

When he arrived he looked down at Cutler, saw his puzzlement. He grinned through the layer of grime. He gestured to the black man and the man stepped back.

'He's Samburu. You'd never pronounce his real name so you can call him Sam.' He attempted to wipe his large right hand on his filthy trousers and extended it. 'I'm Piet van Rensberg' – he pronounced it 'von'. 'You can call me either Pete or Van.'

Cutler sat up, wincing involuntarily, seeing that van Rensberg noted the expression. Piet took Cutler's right arm and helped him to his feet. The strength in the man surprised Deke who shook hands and introduced himself.

'I see my name and accent have you fooled. I'm from Africa, born in the south, but the family moved to Kenya many years ago. We had a cattle farm there – we call them farms but they're very much like your ranches.'

'I've heard of Africa, but not this other place.'

'Kenya. Very beautiful country. A rich land. Sam's people have lived there for centuries. He was kind of a foster-father to me, brought me up while my own father ran the farm and went hunting big game.'

Cutler frowned. Van Rensberg appeared to be about forty. 'He doesn't look that old...'

Sam remained impassive, one bare foot resting behind the knee of his other leg, leaning his weight on the slim, upright spear. Piet laughed.

'You'd be surprised at how old he is. But he doesn't know himself, only roughly. Haven't seen you around here before.'

'Just arrived. Durango Spain's partner.'

Van Rensberg squinted. 'Ah...' was all he said.

Cutler pointed to the short-handled spear. 'I've never seen one like that. Thought at first you'd broken it.'

Piet held up the spear, turning it slowly so that the sun glinted as it ran down the honed edges.

'Assegai. A spear developed by a Zulu king named Shaka in the early 1800s for close in-fighting. Revolutionized war at the time for the Zulus. Very effective weapon once you've mastered it.'

'So I saw.' Deke gestured to the swamp and the dead boar below. 'You do that for sport?'

'Suppose I do. Nothing so honorable as giving the animals a sporting chance or any-thing like that. I just enjoy the fight and the danger. Got myself a cougar a little while back. Killed several boars, a stag in rut, which I may tell you is not at all an experi-ence I wish to repeat. Not with those antlers raking at my innards! In Florida I once fought a couple of alligators, and a Cape buffalo in the Transvaal. Biggest ambition, though, is to tangle with a grizzly. Looking for something new, you know.'

'With that thing? You'd be plumb loco.'

'Eh, man – I'm an expert with the assegai. Even Sam there wouldn't take me on. He'd outdo me in long range. He can drive that spear of his through a four-inch tree, and right in the knothole he aimed at, so I wouldn't want to tangle with him that way. But he wouldn't fight me hand to hand with assegais.'

'Don't reckon I would, either,' Cutler allowed. 'You got a ranch up here?'

'Ay – neighbour to you. Smaller holding. I have men to run the place while I hunt. Take after the old man, I s'spose.'

'Sounds like a nice set-up.'

Van Rensberg grinned.

'I went back to South Africa before America. I ... picked up some diamonds still allowing me to indulge my sport.'

There was something in the way that the man said it that made Cutler think he hadn't come by the diamonds legitimately.

'Well, I'd better get down to the river and wash this filth off me. Care to try some genuine Cape brandy? I have a bottle or two left up at the house...'

'I've never tasted it, but, yeah. I'd like to.'

'Sam'll fetch your horse. If you feel like walking, that is...?' There was a query in Pete's voice and he looked steadily at Cutler.

'I guess I need the exercise.'

'Ah.'

'They call him Dutch Piet round these parts,' Spain said over the supper table after Deke had told him and Karen about his meeting with the strange van Rensberg.

'Ex-army of some sort. From South Africa, he says.'

'Yeah. Lotta Dutchies there, I hear. Keeps to himself. Big *hombre*. Likes to hunt with spears.'

Cutler told them then about the man killing the wild boar in hand-to-hand combat with the assegai.

'It's true then, eh?' Spain said, pursing his lips and shrugging. 'I've heard talk of it. Spends a lotta time over in the Territory, too, hunting bears, they say.'

Karen seemed interested but Deke couldn't tell her much.

'Built like a statue and looks like one – his face I mean. His jaw reminds me of the prow of a sailing ship I saw once in Vera Cruz. Hair grows down low to his eyebrows and he has a large broken nose, What you'd call a strong face.'

'Yes. I've only seen him once but I thought he was – different from other men.' Spain looked at Karen sharply and she smiled, reaching out to touch his hand. 'Oh, no need for jealousy, Durango! You're quite handsome enough for me!'

'I better be,' he growled, the half-grin belying the frown. 'Seems to have a deal of money.'

'Seems to,' Cutler agreed but said nothing about any diamonds. 'Big spread, but the buildings are a bit different from ours – and the ranch kitchen's a separate building – huge, with slate floors and some kind of thatching on the roof. African style he says.'

'A slice of home,' Durango allowed sardonically.

Then they changed the subject and after the meal, sitting out on the porch having a smoke, Durango said casually:

'Dutch mention the Territory at all?'

Cutler was surprised at the question.

'Not really. Said he figured it might be a problem some time for all the ranches along the river.'

'Not for him.'

'What's that mean?'

Spain blew a plume of smoke before answering.

'Word is he deals with the outlaws, lets 'em use his place as a safe trail in and out of the Territory. He's the only one round here who's never lost any cows to rustlers.'

Deke made a point of riding out along the line between Shoestring and van Rensberg's ranch, which, of course he had called *Assegai*, the brand being a short-handled spear.

He had seen the big sprawling ranch house with its riverstone work and heavy log construction and the thatch roof that made it look so out of place here. But he wanted to get a better look at the holdings – and for some reason, felt it would be best if he wasn't seen by Dutch Piet or his riders.

It was just a hunch, probably influenced by Spain's rumour that van Rensberg dealt with the Territory outlaws.

It was nothing new. Deke had known plenty of Border ranchers down on the Rio who did deals with rustlers and *contrabandistas*, turning a blind eye when such men crossed their land on dark and dangerous missions into Mexico.

He had to remember he was no longer a Ranger – but it would be awkward, at the least, to have a neighbour who allowed outlaws to use his land for their forays along the Red River.

He wondered why Spain hadn't looked into it? Likely because he had enough worries trying to make Shoestring pay, he supposed.

Cutler watched the Assegai ranch from high timber, still on Shoestring land, well hidden. But maybe the sun flashed from his field glasses as he focused them on a small tight group of riders heading out from the ranch yard. One man in the lead looked up, seemingly right at him, then, after a hesitation, kept riding, though he dropped back to join the others and two of them also glanced towards the timber where Deke waited.

He decided to let it go for that day but was back the following morning before sun-up, crossing the creek so that he was amongst some boulders that were closer to the trail used by the men. He didn't need field glasses here.

The same small bunch of men rode out and he was able to follow their progress from the boulders until they split up into three groups, two pairs, three men in the other group. Deke smiled faintly: this was making it hard for him, for now he had to decide whom to follow, had to choose one out of three. He could easily pick the wrong one. But the fact that they were taking such precautions told him they were up to something.

He waited, watching. One pair rode out of

sight over a hogback rise. The other pair went down to a small creek and started taking measurements that told Cutler van Rensberg was considering building a small dam – conserving water in these dry conditions was a mighty good idea.

The three other riders were out of sight when he turned to look for them and he couldn't say just where they had gone. It was time to move out, anyway. He clambered down to where he had ground-hitched the grey and was lifting a foot towards the stirrup when the riders appeared, at three different points, covering him with their rifles.

'What you doin' on Mr Rensberg's land, mister?'

The man who spoke had long legs and a chunky body. He sat his saddle easily, thumb on his rifle's hammer. He was bearded but not as if he was growing one permanently, more like he hadn't bothered to shave for a week or so.

'Far as I know, I'm still on Shoestring.'

The chunky man shook his head slowly.

'Creek loops here. You've crossed and recrossed it but it's put you on the wrong side.'

'Well, I'm new to this neck of the woods. My mistake.'

'It is.'

The other two closed in behind him and Cutler turned slowly, to watch them, putting his back to the grey which wouldn't move unless he commanded it to. It gave him something solid and stable behind him – and it forced the chunky man to knee his mount out into the open so he could see Deke clearly.

'Mr Rensberg don't like trespassers.'

'I've met him. My name's Deke Cutler.'

'The Ranger, Lyall,' said a swarthy rider on Cutler's left.

'Not any more,' Deke said quickly.

'Could be. Or could be you're up here workin' under cover,' Lyall said.

'We better take it easy, Lyall,' said the third man worriedly, a lanky ranny with a horselike face.

'Leave this to me, Hoss. Cutler. Know that name. Used to ride the Rio country few years back. You outta the San Angelo Ranger station?'

'I've worked out of there, yeah,' Deke said warily.

'Uh-huh. You led a raid on some fellers bringin' up a big bunch of hosses from Mexico, at the Indio Crossing.'

The name rang bells in Cutler's brain.

'The horses belonged to a rancher name of Felipe Marino, as I recall. Your bunch killed four of his men – and two women who were in the camp of his *caballeros*.'

'Greaser women! There was only me and my half-brother who got out of that gunfight, Ranger! And my brother died two days later from a wound he'd taken at the Crossin'.'

'We gave you all a chance to surrender.'

'Eyewash! Damn Rangers wanted to teach us Border men a lesson. You shot to kill!'

'That's what we were paid for, Lyall. Long time ago. What's it got to do with now?'

The chunky man grinned lifting the rifle.

'First time we've met since, Ranger – you work it out.'

'Hey, Lyall!' shouted the lanky ranny called Hoss. 'I don't want no part of this!'

'Then ride out, damn you! How about you, Leach?'

The swarthy man ran a tongue around his lips. 'Bit chancy, Lyall...'

'You ride out with Hoss then! This feller's trespassin'. I just need you fellers to stick around long enough to swear he went for his gun first before I...'

He thumbed back the rifle's hammer. Then there was a single shot and Lyall rolled back-wards over his horse's rump, his rifle discharging, setting the animal plunging.

Cutler turned his smoking six-gun towards Leach and Hoss, hoping he wouldn't drop the Colt, because his arm felt as if it had been torn up from wrist to elbow and his thumb ached excruciatingly. He had surprised himself with the smoothness and speed of his draw, had reacted instinctively, but his arm was giving him hell with just that one shot. He had to keep a straight face, bite back the pain while he kept them covered. If they thought he couldn't shoot again...

'You gents aiming to buy in?' He hoped his voice didn't betray the fact that he was in agony. The gun started to waver and he tightened his grip, let the barrel move from one man to the other, as if he had meant it to.

They lifted their hands, holding their rifles over their heads.

'We were gonna ride out!' bleated Hoss. 'You heard Lyall tell us to ride out!'

Cutler looked down at Lyall. The man was huddled on his side on the ground. Deke used a boot-toe to roll him on to his back. The bullet had taken him through the middle of the chest.

'He dead?' Leach asked hoarsely.

'Yeah. You'd best tote him back to van Rensberg. Make sure you tell him *exactly* what happened.'

He managed to hang on until they had loaded Lyall on to his horse and they led him away from the boulders and down to the creek. Sagging against a rock, gun holstered, massaging his burning, knotted forearm, Cutler watched them ride away, wondering what sort of reaction the incident would bring from the African.

The thing was, had van Rensberg known that Lyall was a wanted man when he hired him?

Durango Spain wasn't pleased when Cutler reported it to him.

'Why the hell'd you have to kill him?'

'He was going to kill me.'

Spain swore.

'Yeah, well, you always did have a reputation as a killer. Hell, Deke, I know you wouldn't've had any choice, but something like this could get back to the sheriff in Wichita Falls and he might come up and investigate.'

'Nothing to hide,' Cutler said.

Spain's glance was sharp and intense.

'Look. Out here we kind of run things ourselves. We try to keep official law right out of it.'

'This is an ex-Ranger talking? One who earned three bravery awards from the State Governor?'

Durango Spain smiled crookedly.

'Yeah! Kind of strange, ain't it? But ... I guess I've been living here long enough to go along with the way of things, Deke. Different way of life here, makes it easier. We have enough troubles what with the weather and the Injuns.'

'Not to mention Badman's Territory being within spitting distance,' Deke cut in and Spain nodded gently.

'Yeah – sure. But this is wide-open country, Deke. Real wild frontier. Being an *ex*-lawman don't count for spit here – and it don't pay to keep remembering how The Book says things oughta be done. Forget that. That's past now, for both of us. We have to live here, so we have to adapt, live the way everyone else does. Or we ain't gonna live here for long.'

Cutler frowned. He didn't like the sound of that. He knew what Spain meant, but he had noticed his old pard did a lot less smiling than when he had last known him.

Was he imagining it or was there some

kind of veiled warning in Durango Spain's words?

Not that he was going to think too much about it, for his right arm was taking all his attention right now. If he had to draw his six-gun again, this minute, he wouldn't have a hope. The pain was clear up into his shoulder and neck. His ear was ringing wildly, and he felt strange in the head.

'Think I'll go lie down for a spell,' he told the startled Spain abruptly and groped his way back into the house.

His heart was hammering: *hell almighty, if this was how he was going to be, he couldn't figure on lasting long in this Red River country.*

CHAPTER 5

NIGHT RIDERS

Deke Cutler didn't get much sleep although he retired early. He hadn't been in bed long when he heard voices on the porch – and he recognized Piet van Rensberg's thick accent.

He pulled on a shirt and trousers, grimacing every time he moved his arm, and then Karen knocked on the door.

'Deke? Are you awake?'

'I heard Dutch Piet, Karen – I'm coming.'

He wondered whether to strap on his six-gun but decided against it. It wouldn't look friendly for one thing and, anyway, his arm was still too damn sore and swollen to use it. He knew what had happened before, when he had shot Lyall: he had moved too fast and corkscrewed his wrist as he turned to clear the horse. Both the old Indian and Doc Farraday had told him to avoid twisting the forearm for some time. There were still muscles and tendons to heal and there were mangled nerve-ends, too, which could easily get caught up and give him the kind of agony he was now experiencing. There was a solution to it – and he knew he was going to have to try it before long. Unpleasant, naturally, but...

In the parlour, van Rensberg and the big Samburu, with his spear, were waiting. Deke nodded and Piet did the same in reply. Sam, of course, said nothing, just stood impassively, holding his long spear. He had what appeared to be either a short sword or an unusually long and wide-bladed knife in a canvas sheath attached to the belt around his waist. Deke learned later it was called a *panga*, not unlike a machete.

'Pete's here about the man you shot,' Spain said without preamble and Karen frowned at his lack of tact.

'He was going to shoot me.' Cutler looked levelly into the South African's eyes. 'Hoss and Leach might've told you that.'

'Eh, man. They told me they didn't know what had happened. That Lyall seemed to know you from down on the Rio and next thing you shot him.'

'That the way it happened, Deke?' Spain asked. He seemed tense and smoked jerkily.

Deke nodded. 'But Lyall had cocked his rifle hammer, told the other two to ride out

– but to be sure to say they saw me reach for my gun first.'

Van Rensberg smiled thinly. 'Seems you were too fast for them to see any kind of a draw, man.'

'I was shot in my gun arm six months ago. Bullet tore out some muscle and tendons. It doesn't work like it should. Guess I tried a mite too hard, because I not only got my gun out as fast as I've ever used it, but I hurt my arm and it's still giving me pure hell.'

'Thought you looked like you were recovering from something. Well, Lyall's no loss. He was a hard man.'

'You hired him,' Spain said tautly.

Pete's eyes swivelled towards the rancher.

'This is a hard land, Durango. It needs hard men to work it. I've seen some of your ranch crew and I'll bet they don't all go to church on Sundays. Like Ringo, Hal Tripp, that big Jno...'

Spain sighed. 'No, guess not. Like you say, it takes hard men. But you gonna make a stink over Lyall? What I remember about him he was pretty damn mean.'

'He was. No, I just wanted to get things straightened out and make sure it won't happen again.' The cool, pale-blue eyes swept around the room and its occupants.

'Despite what some say around these parts, I *have* been losing cattle. That's why I've told my men to move on anyone found trespassing on my range. Lyall took things a little too far – as you did, Deke – and I'm not saying my orders'll change, but this is just a friendly discussion to clear the air. You all willing to look at it that way?'

Karen said 'yes' right away and nudged Spain but Durango looked at the silent Cutler.

'Deke... ? You were the one got rousted.'

'Be best if you put up some "No Trespassing" signs, Pete, if that's the way you want things,' Cutler said quietly and van Rensberg smiled.

'Guess that's the lawman still in you talking – but why not?'

'Not too damn neighbourly!' Spain snapped.

'Long as we return each other's stock that wanders across the line, I don't see anything wrong.'

Karen placed a hand on her husband's arm.

'I think that's friendly enough, Durango.'

Van Rensberg made a small bow in her direction.

'I thank you, Mrs Spain. Goodnight,

Durango – Deke.' He jerked his head at Sam and the Samburu went out through the door after the big South African like a slim shadow. Karen gave a small shudder.

'That native ... frightens me!'

'He's an odd one,' admitted Spain. 'You see him anywhere around, Karen, you tell me.'

'He's deadly with that spear, Durango,' warned Deke.

'Trick'd be not to get within throwing range,' Spain said with a crooked grin, slapping a hand against his holstered Colt.

Deke felt more uneasy than ever when he went back to bed.

He tossed and turned most of the night, got up and stoked the fire in the kitchen, heated water, soaked his arm in a bowl and it gave him relief. But after only an hour's sleep it woke him again and he got up, dressed and went out to the tool shed attached to the barn.

There was a bench vice there with wooden jaws. He cut a piece of a harness strap and placed the leather between his teeth. Deke put his hand in the vice's jaws which he padded with old rags and slowly tightened them. When they gripped firmly, sweat now squeezing out of his face, he gingerly turned the arm first to the left, then to the right, the wrist joint creaking. Movement was restricted but moving the forearm to the right increased the burning pain and he knew this was where the nerves had pinched.

It was drastic but he knew what he had to do – the Old Indian had done it twice for him out at Big Hat but here he had to prepare himself and then give the short, sharp twist at just the right moment. He balked twice, the pain making him sweat and nauseous, then bit deep into the leather strap and gave the short, snapping wrench as the Indian had shown him. Something went *click* in his wrist.

His left hand instinctively released the pressure of the jaws as he slumped, out cold, knocking over the candle stub and extinguishing it. He floated in limbo for a time and when he started to come round, heard voices, coming from the barn. It was still dark but there was a greyness that told him sun-up wasn't far off. Through the pounding in his head, he recognized Hal Tripp's voice speaking in a hoarse whisper.

'Jimmy.' That would be Jimmy Taggart, the friendly young wrangler. 'Put the mounts away and make sure you rub 'em down first. Don't want no one to know they been ridden hard tonight.'

'Jeepers, Hal, I know what to do!'

'Just makin' sure. And when you got time, bring in some of that hoss liniment. Ringo got ... hurt.'

'Was he shot?' Jimmy asked, fear in his voice.

'Just a nick – nighthawk a mite trigger-happy. Now you be quick, kid... We gotta turn in and grab a little shut-eye, be in our bunks when everyone wakes up.'

Deke must have passed out again for a time, for it was all quiet when he came to. He felt so lousy, he wasn't sure whether he had overheard Tripp and Jimmy Taggart or if he had dreamt it.

He didn't see anyone when he eventually made his way back to his room and fell on to his bed, nursing his still throbbing arm.

'What you aim to do today?' Spain asked Cutler as they had their after-breakfast smokes on the porch. There was activity in the yard as men saddled horses, ready for their chores.

'Gonna start getting myself back into shape,' Deke answered the rancher. 'I'm improving but not fast enough.' He rubbed his right arm. He was bruised around the wrist

75

joint and on the back of his hand. 'Gonna start running along the river, force it a little more each day. Do some work on my gun arm, too, lifting bags of sand, squeezing rubber balls.'

Spain looked at him sharply.

'Expecting trouble?'

'Not looking for it, but if I have to use my six-gun again like I did on Lyall, I don't want to feel crippled afterwards. I couldn't've fired that gun a second time, Durango. I'd've been dead if Leach and Hoss had decided to take me on.'

Spain nodded sympathetically.

'That backshot nearly finished you, didn't it, pard?'

'Came close.'

'Too close, sounds like.' Spain heaved to his feet. 'OK. You get yourself back in good shape and then we'll put you to work.' He grinned. 'Make you earn your keep.'

Then, in case that sounded a little unfriendly, he dug his hand into his pocket and brought out a roll of bills.

'Here. Been meaning to give you this.'

Cutler frowned, not taking the money.

'What is it?'

'I know it bothers you that you ain't paid that sawbones in Big Hat, the one who saved your life. Believe you said you still owed two-hundred fifty bucks. Well, here it is. Take it and send it to him.'

Cutler took it slowly, watching his partner's face. 'I'm obliged, Durango, but I can't take this if things're as tight as you say with the ranch.'

Spain waved it aside.

'You know me. Worrier type. Tend to exaggerate.'

'You ... sure?'

'Hell, yeah!' Spain sounded impatient now. 'I sold a few cows over the last few days to some fellers just getting started on the river. Pay off the sawbones and you can start pulling your weight here with an easy mind.'

'Well, it sure is a surprise.' Then Cutler said, without even planning it: 'Hal Tripp and Ringo handle the deal?'

Durango Spain frowned, his eyes sweeping across Deke's rugged face.

'What the hell makes you say that?'

Deke shrugged.

'Dunno, really. Just got the impression those two were rounding up some cows when I saw them yesterday afternoon. Foothills pasture.'

'Well, they would've been, but no – I handled the deal myself. Feller paid me yesterday afternoon.'

Cutler put the money away.

'Well, thanks again, Durango – I'll make up for this.'

'Take a ride into town and send it off by wire. Then you can relax – and work at your exercises.'

He went down into the yard, calling to some men before they rode out. Deke watched, smoking slowly.

It was a nice gesture. So why did he get the feeling that Spain was kind of mad at him over something?

The running showed him just how much out of shape he really was. After only half a mile he was sweating enough to soak his clothes and breathing like a locomotive with a leaky boiler. He leaned forward, hands on his knees, careful not to put too much pressure on his gun-arm wrist, fighting for breath.

Swinging the arm when he ran made it ache and the wrist was burning again. He hoped the damaged nerves were not going to pinch up on him. Then he got the notion that if he could give the wrist some support, just like when it was sprained from roping or bull-dogging, it might help. So he made a rawhide cuff and laced it tight, having to try several times before he got the pressure and tension just right. Too much and it cut off the blood's circulation. Too little and it didn't give the wrist the support it needed.

But it seemed to work and he changed the rawhide for some stiffer, still pliable leather, cut from an old saddle flap. He made it longer, like an archer's armguard. This was better: he was pleasantly surprised at how much easier it was for him to use his right hand. It helped the arm, the support keeping the nerve ends properly aligned so they didn't pinch and cause numbness and pain. The swelling went down rapidly.

That fixed to his liking, he concentrated on running, forcing himself on for another hundred yards even when he was ready to drop. He overdid it sometimes but after a week he was running two miles without undue distress. At the end of the second week he was doing five and he knew this distance would increase as the weeks went by.

Twice he saw van Rensberg and the Samburu. This was where he learned that Sam's big knife was called a *panga* in Africa and it was used for many things: cutting grass for hut roofs, kindling, wood for fences, defence against wild animals – or wild people.

'Could make a mess of a man,' Deke opined and he caught Pete and Sam exchanging a strange look.

'Could easily take his head off,' van Rensberg allowed. 'Thought I saw some bear tracks.' He gestured up into the hills. They were standing on neutral ground, just beyond where their fences met in a point. 'Not very familiar with the local wildlife. Possible there's a grizzly around here?'

'Never heard of any. Want me to take a look at the tracks?'

'Eh, man, that would be fine!'

Sam never rode anywhere. He trotted alongside his master's big sorrel, sometimes holding to the stirrup strap. They rode up into the hills. When they stopped at the place where Pete had found the tracks, they looked out over a deep bend of the river to slopes and dark-green timber beyond.

'That's the Territory yonder,' Deke said thoughtfully. 'Our line comes closer to it than I thought.'

'Nice country. Here. What do you think?'

Cutler dismounted and went down on to one knee, examining the tracks. They were the size of a saucer. He sat back on his heels and thumbed back his hat.

'He's a big'n, a black, I suspect, and heading for the Territory.'

Excitement glinted in van Rensberg's eyes.

'Hear that, Sam. A big one! A worthy trophy, Deke?'

'Can't say. He might have a coat all tore-up from fighting. He's got a limp, anyway.'

Pete frowned swiftly.

'He's hurt?'

'Might have a thorn in his foot or a stone's worked into his pad. Won't improve his temper.' He squinted at the man. 'You're not going after him with that short spear?'

'The assegai? Only way to do it to my way of thinking. My strength and cunning pitted against his.'

'You prick him with that and he'll tear your head off, then rip up the whole damn county in a bad mood.'

Van Rensberg drew himself up, taller than Deke by a few inches.

'Eh, man, I don't let wounded game slink away to die in agony. I have my pride and honour. If I happen to wound something, I chase it down until I can put it out of its misery. No matter how long it takes or how dangerous it is to me!'

Cutler stared at him as he straightened

and reached for tobacco and papers.

'Take my advice. Take along a shotgun loaded with solid slugs.'

The South African didn't seem to think there was any cause for humour. The way his thick lips clamped, Deke figured the man was mighty mad, fighting to control it. He realized then that Pete had taken his words as a criticism of his courage and dedication to his singular way of hunting and it had stung him.

'I've been fighting and killing wild game for many years, Deke. I'm willing to listen to warnings about how dangerous a certain animal can be, but I will not change my main style. If I get into trouble, Sam will use his spear.'

'Judas, Pete. You don't know what bears are like! This is only a black but they can be plenty mean. If you should happen to run into a grizzly, say around eight feet tall...'

He let the words trail off: van Rensberg was becoming even more excited at the prospect of meeting such a formidable animal.

Deke Cutler left them and rode back to Shoestring land. He hipped in the saddle once and saw they were climbing through the timber across the river in Badman's Territory – or The Nations as a lot of men called the place up here.

Shaking his head, he rode back to the dry wash he had been using for practice with his six-gun.

He was almost back to his old form, fast fluent actions that placed the bullets where he aimed. And he was able to manage it without more than a dull ache in his wrist and arm.

He figured he was now about ready to tackle the worst that this Red River country could throw at him. And that included the wild men who inhabited the Territory.

It was time to go to work and really pull his weight around here.

After shooting six egg-sized stones off the top of a rock at the end of the dry wash, the Colt empty and smoking, feeling comfortable in his hand now, he heard the horses coming.

It was too late to reload and he had the notion that this trio of beard-shagged, dirty-looking riders had waited until this moment to make their appearance.

They had guns out, two with rifles, one with a six-shooter. They stopped their mounts a few yards from where he stood, his grey nearby with trailing reins. He had been working on the animal so that it didn't shy or spook at gunfire, bringing it a little closer to his gun each day. Now he reckoned he could shoot from the saddle and the animal wouldn't flinch. His own rifle was in its scabbard but on the far side of the horse.

He allowed he had been in less dangerous situations than this one.

Deke nodded curtly.

'Howdy, gents. Don't b'lieve I've seen you round before. Which spread you with?'

The one with the six-gun was slightly ahead of the others. He was big and dirty and his hat had a floppy brim with ragged edges. His clothes, like the others, were patched roughly, worn through in places. Deke knew these were men who lived wild – and wouldn't work for a ranch under any circumstance.

They would rather toss a wide loop over someone else's cattle. These were men from the outlaw territory across the river.

'We work for ourselves, mister,' the man in the ragged hat said, jerking the Colt. 'Might's well drop that empty gun. It ain't gonna do you no good.'

Instead of dropping it, Deke replaced it in his holster. They didn't like that: they wanted to be obeyed.

Ragged Hat heeled his mount forward. 'Like the look of your hoss, mister,' he said, 'and likely I'll take it with me when I go, but we'll give you a choice. Been watchin' you shoot. Like to have you with us, join our bunch and help us hit the ranches along the river. You could get rich.'

'Or dead,' Deke said, shaking his head. 'I'll pass, friend.'

The man stopped his horse a couple of feet short of Cutler, glanced at his companions.

'Now how'd I know all along he was gonna say somethin' just like that?'

'Reckon he's just got that kinda look, Salty,' chuckled one man, short but solidly built. The third man, small in every way and older, spat on Deke's saddle.

'Uh-huh. You boys're out for trouble, eh?'

Salty grinned, showing gapped, yellow teeth. 'Well, you sure ain't gonna give us any!'

And he jumped his mount forward, swinging with his gun at Deke's head. Except Cutler was no longer standing where he had been. He spun between Salty's horse and the grey, grabbed the outlaw's leg and heaved him out of the saddle. The man yelled and the ragged hat rolled away down slope, revealing Salty's bald dome.

As he slid and skidded, the other two worked their mounts, trying to get a shot at Deke who dived under his horse and came up on the other side, reaching for his rifle. They triggered and dirt exploded around Cutler's boots but he had the rifle now, jumped back from the grey and thrust the gun over the saddle, levering and triggering. The older, short man was standing in his stirrups, looking for a clear shot at Cutler. The first bullet snapped his head back and hurled him from the saddle. The solid built man was hanging over the side of his horse in the Indian fighting position, levering and shooting under the racing animal's arched neck.

Cutler's lead cut him down and dropped the horse, too, and man and animal skidded and rolled down-slope.

Salty, dazed, was on his feet and shooting wildly as he started to run up the slope. One bullet struck Deke's saddle horn and he reared back, stung by pieces of flying, torn leather. His boots slipped in the gravel and the grey twitched and moved away a couple of feet, exposing him.

Salty stopped, baring his teeth as he drew bead on the helplessly floundering Cutler.

Deke put down a hand to push off the slope, still gripping the rifle in his right hand – and then froze as Salty gave a blood-chilling cry.

When Cutler looked in the outlaw's direction, he saw Salty's dirty body sagging forward over the long glittering spear-shaft that pinned him to a pine tree, the oval blade right through the centre of his chest.

CHAPTER 6

DEAD MEN RIDING

Spain was working with Jimmy Taggart and the big, surly cowhand called Jno, branding maverick calves in the yard, when Cutler rode in. He was weary despite his improved stamina and it showed in the deep vertical channels drawn in his flesh around his mouth.

Spain looked up, coughing a little in the burnt-hair smoke as yet another bawling calf staggered to its feet and joined its protesting companions in the smallest corral.

'You been gone a long time.'

'Almost didn't make it back.' Those words got the attention of all three men as Deke dismounted stiffly. 'Doing some shooting with the six-gun in a draw when three hardcases from the Territory set on me.'

He was watching Spain closely but it was Jno who asked harshly:

'How you know they was from the Territory? There's lots of riders use them hills.'

'It was at the sharp bend of the river. Didn't realize how close to the Territory line our land comes.'

'No? Thought I showed you on the map. Nothing to worry about. Ringo was a little unlucky but usually they keep to themselves, the men over there.'

'Didn't this time. Heard my shooting and came on down. Were aiming to take my horse and everything else, I guess.'

Spain's eyes narrowed.

'*Were?* You kill 'em all?'

'Got two.'

'What happened to the third one?'

'He got himself speared, pinned to a white pine, right through the heart.'

The three men were silent. 'Injuns!' said Jimmy Taggart after a pause. 'They reckon the tribes are all gettin' together an' there's gonna be hell to pay once they get guns...'

Deke shook his head.

'No, Jimmy. Dutch Pete's sidekick. The Samburu.'

'That lanky devil?' asked Jno. 'Goddamn, I knew that son of a bitch'd end up killin' someone.'

'Glad he did. I slipped and the outlaw would've nailed me if Sam hadn't speared him.'

89

'What the hell was he doing on Shoestring?' Spain asked quietly, looking hard at Deke.

'Saw him and Pete earlier down by the river at the point where our fences meet. They'd found a bear's tracks and crossed into the Territory. Pete wanted to run it down and fight it with his assegai.'

'Christ! Man must have a death wish,' opined Jno.

'Maybe. Anyway they lost the tracks and crossed the river a little higher than they meant to. Put them on our land. They heard the shooting and came on down. Like I said, I'm mighty glad they did.'

'Uh-huh.' Spain continued to watch Cutler's face. 'You don't seem to have much luck with the fellers from north of the river, Deke. This is twice now.'

Deke nodded, returning Spain's searching gaze.

'Yeah. I recognized two of them. Didn't at first, but when I took a good look after they were dead, I saw who they were – Salty Shaw and that old hellion they called Twist. You recollect him, Durango? He'd use women on a raid and then twist their necks....' He watched his partner closely now, waiting.

Spain was very tense.

'Can't be, Deke,' he said very slowly. 'Neither Twist nor Salty. They were both killed down on the Rio. Hell, you knew that, didn't you?'

'Thought I did. I *knew* there was something queer about 'em. But they must be twins to the others, one even going by the name of Salty – we buried 'em out there.'

Spain said nothing, just stared.

Deke shrugged. 'Must've been mistaken, I guess.'

'You must've. Why don't you go on up to the house? Karen'll make you some coffee. Or there's whiskey in the sideboy if you feel the need for something stronger.'

'Yeah, I'll do that. Where's Hal Tripp and Ringo, by the way?'

Spain frowned. 'Out chousing mavericks. Why?'

'Nothing. Just that Dutch Pete said he thought he saw them riding into a draw across in the Territory.'

'Well, could be. If they figured there were some mavericks worth going after.'

'Kinda dangerous, ain't it?'

Spain shrugged. 'I don't like the boys doing it but if it's gonna pay off, why not chance it?'

'I'd want danger money.'

'Hell, I don't *send* 'em over. It's their own choice, so no extra pay. Satisfied?' Spain's voice was tight, his face almost belligerent, challenging.

Deke nodded and walked towards the house without speaking, carrying his rifle in his left hand. His right wrist and forearm were a little sore but he was mighty pleased – a couple of weeks back and he'd have been in pure agony. Or lying dead out in the hills.

Karen was solicitous when he told her about the outlaws jumping him – and how he'd thought he recognized them.

'Must've been mistaken, though. Durango said both those fellers were killed down on the Rio when he was still in the Rangers. He said he even shared in the reward because it was put up by cattlemen who'd lost women to that pair; made him eligible to claim, it being private money.'

Karen seemed uncomfortable and avoided looking at him, finding some dishes to re-wash so that her back was to Deke.

'I suppose when men are living wild like that, all dirty and bearded, it's hard to be *sure* of their identity.'

'Guess you're right.' Deke sipped his coffee, laced with Spain's whiskey. 'It was a long time ago. I recollect now Durango used part of that bounty for our deposit on this place.'

'Yes, I seem to recall. Deke, you look a lot fitter now. I'm glad for you. I was afraid for a time that you might not recover for many months.'

'It's been plenty long enough.' He knew she was deliberately changing the subject but he went along with her and soon they were talking about the days before she had married Durango and she even admitted that for a time she thought Deke was going to ask for her hand first.

He smiled ruefully.

'Won't say it didn't cross my mind,' he admitted, cursing the slight flush he felt rising in his gaunt face. 'But I could see the way you two looked at each other...'

She turned from the clay sink, face sober.

'But you didn't notice the way I – looked – at you?'

He felt that tightening in his belly at her words.

'I guess I didn't.'

He let it go at that and he saw some disappointment on her face. *What the hell was this? He had considered asking Karen to marry him once, but figured she would say 'no'*

93

because he still had almost a year to serve in the Rangers, whereas Durango was already out and offering her a home on the Red River...

Now – was she letting him know she might have preferred – him...?

He thrust the thought from him. She was married now to Spain, his partner in Shoestring. Whatever might have been was long gone and couldn't be regained – or *wouldn't* be. His personal code wouldn't allow it, no matter what....

But he felt it was a rising complication and one he could well do without. But ... one he might have to deal with.

The candle on the end of Spain's scarred desk in the ranch office flickered and Cutler glanced up from his study of one of the account books.

He stiffened when he saw the door was ajar and then Karen Spain slid into the room, closing the door softly behind her. She wore a gown over her nightdress and there was a scarf tied around her hair. She didn't seem surprised to find Cutler at the desk, ranch books open before him.

'You only had to ask if you wanted to see the accounts, Deke.' She sounded a trifle stiff.

'I did. Weeks ago. Durango's been fobbing me off one way and another and I got lost in building myself up and let it slide.' He stood and looked down at her as she approached. 'Then tonight my arm was giving me a little trouble, disturbing my sleep, just enough to wake me a few times. I heard horses being saddled at the corrals, saw Durango and Tripp ride out. I kind of thought Ringo might be with them, but I guess his wound was giving him trouble.'

She held his gaze, face sober, then sighed and sat down in a chair opposite the desk.

'How did you know about that?'

'Overheard him one night I was in the barn trying to straighten out my arm.'

'You ... do get around, Deke. I suppose being a Ranger all those years, it's hard not to snoop.' She said it tight-lipped, her gaze cool.

'Wasn't snooping, Karen. Quite a bit of night-riding being done from here, it seems.'

'Durango arranges ... deals, and sometimes they're best done at night.'

'Over in the Territory?'

She hesitated, teeth tugging at her bottom lip.

'Why not ask him when he comes back, Deke? He'll explain – if he wants to.'

He nodded. 'That's just it. There seems to be a helluva lot that's not being explained to me. I have the feeling I arrived before Durango wanted me here. He hasn't exactly put out the welcome mat. If he's dealing with outlaws, as I suspect–'

'Suspect! You've never really stopped being a Ranger have you?' She sounded bitter. But he said nothing and eventually she added: 'Durango nearly drove me mad when we were first married. He couldn't stop acting like a Ranger, poking his nose into everyone's business, warning them about breaking the law. It almost got him killed a couple of times until I put my foot down – hard. Then he seemed to realize that all that law business was behind him now and he had to keep it there. He was a *rancher* now, in near-lawless country, and he had to adapt to that. If it meant shaving the edge of the law, now and then, up here that was – acceptable.'

Cutler was seated behind the desk now and he watched her closely, saw that this was something she had apparently wanted to get off her chest for some time.

'You convinced him of that?'

Her eyes blazed.

'He convinced himself I just wanted him

to feel more at ... ease!' She steadied her breathing. 'We had a lot of arguments, Deke – some about you – and things weren't so rosy for a long time. Then, when he started to lose cattle and fences were torn down and there were outlaws trailing through here – Shoestring land, I mean – he suddenly saw that he had to bend to the Red River way of life – or quit. Or, worse, be killed.'

Deke tapped the books.

'Well, I can't make head nor tail of these. I'd just about decided Durango had fixed things that way to bamboozle the banks. Now I'm sure of it.'

She coloured some, toyed with the robe's tie.

'Deke, you'd best ask Durango for any more details. I've probably said too much already. It's not really my business.'

'Well, I'd say you played a big part in Durango's decision, whatever it was.'

She frowned.

'Why do you say ... that?'

'There's the piano – the floor and wall rugs – the furniture. All had to be shipped from back East if I don't miss my guess. Glass in every window. Hell, Karen, that's almost un-heard of even in some of the bigger towns!'

Karen's face was angry now.

'D'you think I haven't earned those things? Those small ... comforts? You have absolutely no idea of what it's like for a woman out here! I'm not some farm girl who's used to hard living and could easily adapt! You know damn well I come from a good family and – well, I didn't listen to them, of course, but they warned me I would find it – difficult. And *they were right!* I had some dreadful times early in our marriage. I – I really don't know how I coped.'

'But then Durango showed you there could be some rewards, huh?'

'I wish you wouldn't sound so damn ... smug! I know I was spoilt before Durango swept me off my feet and – I was terrified, Deke! Living way out here kept me in a constant state of terror and worry! Indians, drunken, half-crazy outlaws turning up on the doorstep night and day. I was left here so much ... alone!'

He nodded in understanding. 'Yeah, it must've been tough for you, Karen. I guess you thought you had to do all you could to change things. But did you have to push Durango into bending the law? Something he'd risked his life to uphold for all those years? No wonder he never seems happy.'

She stood swiftly, hands clasped and

twisting the cord in front of her.

'You're trying to make me feel guilty!'

'Yes, I am. Durango Spain was one of the finest Rangers ever and he taught me all I know and it saved my neck many a time – but basic to it all, was his code: don't bend the law unless it's to end some lawlessness; don't sell out for a dollar or a thousand dollars; live by your Ranger's oath no matter what. That way you'll keep your pride. I've tried to do that and I'm damn sure Durango did, too. Until...'

She was flushed deep red now and there was a glint of moisture in her eyes.

'I *know,* damn you I *know* all that! It was one of the things I admired about Durango – *and* you! But – I was at my wit's end, Deke! I felt as if I was falling apart! Durango was working desperate hours, killing himself and getting nowhere and we were losing our marriage...'

'Yeah, well, I guess it wouldn't be hard to start looking around for an easy way out when things were that bad.'

'You – you understand that?' She sounded surprised.

'Guess so, Karen, I can't judge you. I just wish Durango hadn't taken that step across the line–'

'Oh, Deke, it's not a big step! Just a few small arrangements now and again. Just about everyone up here does it. Durango says they have to or they won't survive. The outlaws will simply wipe them out.'

He knew that wasn't true: if everyone was involved doing deals with the outlaws, there wouldn't be any need to wipe anyone out.

'D'you know where he's gone now?'

'He and Hal are meeting some men. It's to do with allowing them to drive some steers across our land. Down in the west pasture there's a lot of flatrock and trees beyond the rocks.'

'Hard to track,' opined Deke, half-aloud.

'It's close to a secret canyon or valley across the river where the outlaws hold their cattle until they can get rid of them. Deke, Durango's not involved in the actual rustling.'

'If he lets stolen stock cross his land and does nothing about it, he's a rustler, Karen.'

Her eyes pinched down.

'Damn you, Deke! Don't you turn on him! *Please* don't! I – don't think he could take that...'

She stood directly in his path as he started for the door. He could smell her bath soap on her and he stepped back.

'I've told you how things are, Deke,' she said steadily. 'I don't care if you believe me or not – but – please be careful. Durango's been under a lot of strain lately. Give him a break! *Please!* He's had it hard up here and – it can be a dangerous land, this Red River.'

He said nothing, took her shoulders lightly between his hands and stood her to one side. Then he hurried out into the night.

Shortly after, she heard him riding his grey out of the ranch yard. She bit her lip, hands clasped, crying silently.

She had known that Cutler would find out soon enough that Durango was dealing with the outlaws. All she had tried to do was to ease him into acceptance of the idea.

But now she was afraid she had made a mistake. Deke Cutler was still a Ranger, whether he wore a badge or not. He was a hard, decent man and she knew he had been hurt by the knowledge that Durango Spain, a man he had looked up to for many years, had feet of clay.

What she was afraid of now was, just what Deke was going to do about it.

CHAPTER 7

OUTLAW TERRITORY

Cutler knew he would never find any hidden canyons in the dark – maybe not even in full daylight, come to that – but he had a general direction and worked from the west pasture.

He crossed the river and found the large area of flatrock with the clump of dark trees looming against the stars beyond. The rifle came noiselessly out of the scabbard and he worked the lever swiftly, yet quietly, sliding a cartridge into the breech. He lowered the hammer which had cocked with the lever action, shucked another .44/40 cartridge from his bullet belt and pushed it through the loading gate in the brass side-plate of the rifle. That gave him a full magazine, plus an extra one already in the breech. The old Ranger caution was still working – one extra shot could make the difference between living and dying.

Riding out, he had been thinking about Karen: he hadn't allowed himself to think about her much since her marriage to Durango Spain. Maybe some folk would say he had been too slow, or had left his moves too late, but the fact was he deliberately hadn't made any moves at all or given any sign of how he felt about her. Spain was courting her and Deke hadn't come along until later. In his book and by his code, that gave Spain first claim. She had agreed to marry Durango and had married him. That was an end to any thoughts of romance between Karen and Cutler as far as he was concerned.

Now he found himself feeling sorry for her: he savvied how she must have felt, coming from a rich family in Denver, winding up on the Red River, without a single one of the comforts she was accustomed to. It would seem no great deal to someone in Karen's position for Spain to make 'arrangements' with law-breakers: she had tried to rationalize it by saying Spain wasn't a rustler, but after taking the first bribe to look the other way while rustled beef was driven across his land he was no less an outlaw than the thieves themselves in Deke's book. But if that was Durango's only involvement – and Deke hoped like hell it was — then there was a chance he could get him out before he found himself dragged in any deeper.

At least it explained Durango's cool, disappointing welcome: he hadn't been expecting Deke after hearing rumours of his death and maybe he was fooling himself, but Cutler liked to think that Durango had been trying to protect him by not taking him into his confidence and involving him in any suspect deals. *That* would be like the old Durango Spain he had known and admired for over ten years.

But that didn't mean the men Spain was meeting tonight would have any such inclinations. They might see him only as a Ranger: 'Once a Ranger, always a Ranger – and never a man!', was the credo of some of these hardbitten outlaws – and so they would as soon see him dead to be on the safe side as to accept him as Spain's partner in any deal they had made.

'Hold it, you! Who the hell are you?'

The voice came out of darkness as thick as a blanket in an airless cellar, but Deke thought the owner was somewhere in those trees.

He reined up, still holding the rifle across his thigh one-handed, thumb easing back the hammer, finger curled around the trigger and bringing it back at the same time. Now all he had to do was lift his thumb from the hammer spur and it would fall and fire the cartridge in the breech. It was an old gunfighter's trick, shaving a split second, and he had used it on two previous occasions successfully.

He was ready to try a third time if necessary.

'I asked who the hell you are, mister!' the impatient voice snapped and Deke heard the ratchet of a cocking gun hammer. 'You got about two seconds to say!'

'Looking for Durango Spain.'

'Never heard of him!' Deke didn't say anything and after a short silence the hidden man snapped: 'Why?'

'If you don't know him, it don't matter.'

'Smart-mouth son of a bitch! You'd be Cutler, is my guess.' Deke didn't say one way or the other. 'Goddamnit, answer me! I got my gun trained on you!'

Deke rowelled with his spurs abruptly, falling loosely across his horse's neck as it leaped forward, swinging the rifle out to one side and shooting one-handed into the darkness of the trees. He didn't hold out much hope of finding a target but it would distract the man in there.

He heard the bullet slap against a tree

trunk and saw a vague whiteness that likely was a piece of bark torn away. He thought he heard the tail end of a startled curse but couldn't be sure with the echoing gunshot – followed swiftly by one from the guard. But the man had fired in uncontrolled reaction and his shot was wild.

By that time, Deke had a fresh shell in the breach and was thundering into the line of trees, using knees to guide the grey, although it had popped enough mavericks out of brush-choked draws and on timberline slopes to instinctively start dodging and weaving. A gun hammered again and Deke saw the flash to his left and slightly ahead. He lifted the rifle as he reared up in the saddle and fired.

He could just make out the man falling in there and then he heard the swish of a low-swinging branch. He ducked flat but not quite fast enough. It raked his back and thrust him sideways in the saddle. The horse stumbled as it swerved with the unexpected transfer of weight and cannoned off a tree, adding to the momentum of Cutler's falling body.

He struck the ground heavily, losing the rifle, bounced and rolled. Then the night exploded in a fountain of stars as his head struck the same tree that had sent his horse floundering.

He fell into spinning darkness.

'Goddammit, I told you he wasn't to be killed! Or even shot at!'

The familiar angry voice filtered through Cutler's returning consciousness and he lay wherever he was, trying to recover his senses fully.

'Thing is, Durango, you don't have as much to say around here as you think you do.'

Cutler didn't recognize that voice at first: it was tough and cold and menacing.

'You could be wrong, Flash.' *That could be Flash Bill Danton! An outlaw long supposed dead along the Rio...* 'That trail across my land is the best one available to you.'

A harsh, wet-sounding laugh. *By hell! It was Flash Bill! He was always troubled by a cough!*

'Now you wouldn't be threatenin' me, Durango, ol' hoss, would you?'

'Me? Hell, no. But if the trail was closed to you, you'd have to run the gauntlet of crossing the Red in the open and the Federals are getting more and more patrols along the unsettled stretches – using the army, too, I hear.'

The wet cough came, followed by some hawking, then a brief silence.

'Durango, when you gonna admit you're no longer a Ranger, no longer the boss, and you don't get your own way just because of a couple of stupid threats?'

'Flash, I don't want Cutler hurt. He's had it rough and I can ease him along, but not if someone's trying to blow his head off every time he leaves Shoestring's pastures. *You're* the one ought to be learning a lesson. You counted your dead men lately? And that one he just shot down in the timber. He'll be lucky if he's walking without crutches a month from now. You oughta realize just who it is you're dealing with.'

Cutler opened his eyes and took in his situation. It did little to make him feel any better and it sure didn't help his throbbing head.

There was some kind of a temporary camp, a small fire burning, and he could smell coffee and beans. He could recognize Durango and Hal Tripp and there were three other dark shapes, all bearded as far as he could tell. At first he thought his hands were bound but it was just that he had been lying on them. His right arm was painful but nothing he couldn't bear. He fought to sit up and the movement got the attention of the men around the fire.

They said nothing, let him struggle up, holding one side of his head which was swollen. He felt a crust of dried blood where the skin had broken. Cutler swayed, surprised that he was still wearing his own six-gun. His rifle lay only a couple of feet away, scratched and stone-dented on the butt-stock from its fall. He started to stoop – carefully – to pick it up, but Flash Bill spat and shook his head.

'Nope. Just leave it, Cutler.'

'You're about the healthiest looking ghost I've ever seen, Flash,' Deke grated, but he was looking at Durango who kept his face carefully blank.

'What the hell're you doing here, Deke?' Spain asked and there was an edge of concern in his voice. 'D'you have to poke your nose into every blamed thing?'

'That's the way you taught me, Durango.' Cutler's words were short and cutting, his eyes bleak. 'Anyway, if my pardner keeps sending our men on night rides, or goes himself, I reckon I've a right to know what's going on.'

There was more silence, broken only by the crackle of wood on the fire. Cutler walked forward, hunkered down and poured himself a tin cup half-full from the blackened and battered pot resting on stones at the edge of the flames. It tasted like carbolic but it was hot and he felt it coursing through him.

'Could be dangerous knowledge, Cutler,' growled Danton. The other two outlaws were watching Deke closely, hands on their guns.

'I'm not a Ranger now,' Deke told them. 'I'm going into the cattle-ranching business and I need to know the situation. Looks to me, Durango, like we're dealing with a bunch of owlhoots.'

Spain poked idly at the fire with a twig.

'I'm making the deals. You're not involved.'

Deke snorted. 'You're my *pardner*, for Chris'sakes! How can I not be involved?'

'Because I say you're not. You've a lot to learn about making a living in this country, Deke. You think it was easy for me to start dealing with ... something like this?'

'Watch your mouth, Spain!' growled Flash Bill. His six-gun came up with the flashing speed that had earned him his nickname.

It didn't seem to bother Durango and Cutler looked relaxed but there was a tension across his shoulders and a new alertness in his eyes as he sipped the coffee.

Spain waved away Danton's threatening words.

'Just talking, Flash. No offence.' He suddenly heaved to his feet and Danton and his two men scrambled up quickly. Hal Tripp got up more slowly, looking mighty uneasy. 'Relax. Deke, we better head on back. I've done my business here. Nothing for you to do – unless you want to tell that feller you shot you're sorry.'

'Sorry I didn't nail him dead centre,' Cutler said easily, tossing the dregs of coffee into the fire. It hissed and steam rose. Still getting up, lifting his rifle, Cutler clanged the barrel against the battered pot. It fell, the ill-fitting lid flew off and the liquid and grounds still in it all but extinguished the fire which hissed like a couple of maddened snakes.

The sudden sharp drop in light and the roiling steam confused the others and Cutler moved swiftly, his rifle barrel swinging in a tight arc. It knocked Danton's gun from his grasp, then lifted to slam the man across the side of the head. Flash stumbled into the bearded outlaw next to him and Cutler smashed the butt into this man's forehead. The third outlaw was only now bringing up his six-gun and Spain instinctively kicked it

111

from his hand. Cutler drove the rifle barrel into his midriff and he collapsed to his knees, doubled-up, gagging.

Hal Tripp was looking round bewilderedly, gun half-drawn, waiting for a cue from Spain. Durango turned angrily towards Cutler.

'Goddammit, Deke! What the hell...!'

Cutler ignored him, strode across to Flash Bill and hooked a boot-toe under the dazed man's shoulder. He heaved him on to his back and Danton glared up through pain-dulled eyes. Deke planted a boot in the middle of the outlaw's chest and leaned his weight on it. Danton began to cough painfully.

'I see you or anyone riding for you on Shoestring land, I'll kill you, Flash. We never did get along and from what I recollect, I ought to damn well put a bullet in you right now and save everyone a lot of trouble. You just mind my words – all deals are off!'

'Now wait just one goddamn minute!' snapped Spain, stepping forward. 'You don't speak for me, Deke! This is something you know nothing about and we better get it straightened out between us. Right now!'

'No, not right now. We can sit down and you can tell me just what the hell's been going on, Durango, back at the ranch. But for now, all bets are off. And I meant what I said about shooting on sight.'

'Best sleep with a gun under your pillow, Cutler!' gritted Danton, wheezing and coughing.

'Aw, shut up, Flash!' Cutler said tiredly and kicked the outlaw in the temple. The others were still dazed and groggy and no threat. The man he had wounded down in the trees was lying under a shallow overhang of rock, moaning, not interested in anything but Cutler's bullet which had shattered the bone in his lower left leg.

'Get the horses and let's ride, Durango.'

Spain's face was pale and bleak.

'You holding that gun on me?'

'I am.'

Spain sighed, let his six-gun fall back into its holster and Hal Tripp lifted his hands out from his sides.

'You're gonna regret this, Deke.'

'Well, let's go regret it down at Shoestring. Hal, you bring my grey over here, then both you and Durango lie face down on the ground until I'm mounted.'

Spain's look of hatred was an almost tangible thing.

Deke Cutler remained deadpan.

CHAPTER 8

THE REAL REASON

Cutler didn't see any signal pass between Spain and Tripp but they made a concerted effort to jump him during the river crossing.

He was ready for it – he'd already figured this was the best place to try something if they wanted to.

They both made out that their mounts were shying after they plunged down the broken bank, and although they were behind Cutler, they were one each side of him. He heard the grunt and a smothered *ya-ha!* as they spurred their mounts forward, hoping to catch his grey between them.

Cutler rowelled, too, and the grey, one of the best fast-response horses he had ever owned, and well used to rounding up cattle under all conditions, whinnied slightly and jumped. The result was that Spain and Tripp cannoned into each other. Deke wheeled the grey in a tearing surge of muddy water and it sprang into the pair of whinnying, protesting mounts, knocking both men out of the saddles. Cutler leaned down in the pale light of pre-sun-up, scooped up the trailing reins, turned the grey and kept going across the river, swimming all three horses in the deep middle.

There were shouts of alarm behind him, interspersed with curses, and he instinctively ducked as a gun went off. Looking back, he saw Spain floundering while Hal Tripp had moved back into the shallows and was trying to fire his six-gun again. But it was an old cap-and-ball: he had been lucky to get off that single shot after the drenching in the river.

By then Cutler was climbing the grey up the far bank. The other two mounts, whose reins he had released now, clambered out of their own accord. He unsheathed his rifle, levered in a shell, and raised it to his shoulder.

'Start swimming, boys!'

'Goddamn you to *hell* Deke!' shouted Spain, spluttering, his hat all askew and droopy after its ducking. 'I wish that McKittrick kid *had* killed you!'

'If wishes were horses, Durango. Come on. You brought it on yourselves. Or would you rather stay put, on the wrong side of the river, with drowned six-guns – and likely Flash Bill and his cronies already looking for you?'

Swearing, they waded out as far as they could, muddy water up to their necks, and then floundered their way across. Tripp panicked in the deep water and Deke threw him a rope. In the end, he pulled them both ashore by rope. They sagged on the bank, panting, spewing river water, too weary to even work up their hatred for him.

But they weren't finished with him. When they dismounted at the corrals in the ranch yard, they waited until he off-saddled and threw his rig over the top rail, then they jumped him, co-ordinating their movements. Tripp drove his weight against Cutler and slammed him into the rails. At the same time, Spain hit him in the kidneys and, as Deke sagged, hit him again in the middle of the back.

Cutler's legs gave way and he slid to his knees. Hal Tripp, dander up now, moved in and lifted a knee towards Cutler's face. Deke twisted aside, took the knee on the right shoulder. It hurt and it spun him half-way around, slamming him back into the lower rails of the corral. Tripp moved in with boots swinging but Spain thrust him back, yelling,

'No boots! *No boots!*'

'Hell with you!' Tripp growled and started to swing a kick.

Spain hooked him in the ribs and, as the man doubled over, grabbed his lank, wet hair and ran him head first into a corral post. Tripp fell, unconscious.

Meantime, Deke had gotten his breath back and he saw that Spain was ready for him again, fists lifted as he stepped in over Hal's prone body. Deke hurled a handful of gravel into the rancher's face and Durango staggered, clawing at his eyes. Cutler pulled himself properly to his feet by the rails, lifted a knee into his partner's chest. Spain flew back, hitting the rails. His boots skidded and he slipped, the back of his head rapping hard.

Cutler closed, fists hammering, arms working, turning his shoulders behind the blows, using his weight. Early risers amongst the crew came out of the bunkhouse, shouting at the others still crawling out of their bunks.

'Fight! Fight!'

The men crowded outside, yelling, some swinging punches at the air as they ducked and weaved in time with the two men who seemed intent on knocking each other's head off. Both men were bleeding from facial cuts and their shirts were ripped. Deke fended a clubbing blow aimed at his nose, twisted his lean body and used all his weight as he slammed a hard fist into Spain's ribs. Durango grunted and looked grey and sick as he jack-knifed, clutching at his midriff. He was hurt and he back-pedalled, covering his head with his arms as Cutler stalked him, watching for an opening, ripping in blows with the speed of a striking diamondback. Spain lurched as each blow landed. He wobbled unsteadily, fighting back by pure instinct, sometimes seeming only to try to *push* away the knotted fists that were reducing him to a battered wreck.

Deke was surprised: he had seen Durango in dozens of fist fights over their years in the Rangers, and Spain had had the stamina of an elephant, knocking down man after man and hardly breathing more heavily than if he had been playing poker, standing with his victims piled up around him, knee-deep.

Now, a few minutes of hard slogging, a couple of haymakers, and a faceful of straight lefts, and Durango Spain was about ready to give up. *No!* No, he wouldn't give up, no matter how bad he was hurt. He would take all the punishment that was thrown at him and finally go down, maybe, but no man would ever hear him cry *'Nough!*

There was something wrong! Deke, breathing plenty hard from his exertions, slowed down as the thought struck him, startled, unable to believe what he was seeing. Spain had always seemed a certainty to win any fight that might have started between them while they were in the Rangers but it had never happened, out of mutual respect for one another.

Now...

Both men jumped as a rifle crashed and one of the corral rails shuddered as a bullet slashed a foot-long sliver from it. As they crouched, turning towards the house, the rifle fired again and the bullet exploded gravel from the ground between them.

'Hey!' gasped Spain, lifting a hand towards the porch where Karen stood with the smoking gun – already levering a third shell into the breech. 'Karen! What – the – *hell* – you think – you're – doing?'

'Stopping you two fools from killing each other!' The rifle was at her shoulder now, aiming between them, ready to shift to one or the other. 'Now, back away. Get at least three feet between you – and keep your hands down at your sides! *Do it!*'

They did it. She nodded in satisfaction, glanced towards the bunched crew outside the bunkhouse. 'You men get your breakfast and go about your chores.'

Mumbling, the ranch hands moved away, most starting to grin, some pantomiming the fight; there would be plenty of talk over breakfast this morning.

'Now you two – wash up in the horse trough and then come into the kitchen. There'll be no breakfast for either of you until we settle this thing ... whatever it is!'

She turned back into the house and Deke glanced at the bloody Spain who was still fighting for breath, holding his ribs. If *he* looked as bad, it was no wonder he felt as if he had been caught up in a stampede, Deke allowed silently.

'You might've told me you'd taught her how to shoot!'

'Just as – well I – did – or she'd have – blown our – damn heads – off!'

They linked arms and staggered across to the horse trough.

Breakfast was mainly silent and both Deke and Durango had a little trouble eating the meal because of swollen jaws and tender gums. Karen had treated their cuts and scrapes – and given them a tongue-lashing while she was doing it.

'A pair of fools!' she began, making Spain wince and suck in his breath as she dabbed at a deep cut above his left eye. 'I don't think I've ever seen two grown men act so like dirty-faced school boys as much as you two!'

'Now, listen, Karen,' slurred Spain indignantly, but an extra dab of iodine into the cut choked off his words and she started in again.

'You haven't seen each other in over a year. You, Durango, didn't get the small but steady income you were hoping for so you pushed Deke off to one side – as if he wasn't here! Not just like another hired hand: that would've been bad enough, but just to virtually ignore him, pretend he wasn't around...'

'Aw, it wasn't that bad,' Cutler said and withered a little at the look she tossed at him.

'And *you!* Half-dead, weak, desperate to know what was going on, couldn't forget you were no longer a Ranger and started poking your nose into Durango's business and got his back up even more! Didn't you know him well enough when you spent all those years together in the Rangers to see that he was only trying to keep you out of... things – so you wouldn't get into trouble?'

Spain brightened briefly. 'Yeah! *That's* why I tried to keep him out of it, love–'

'You be quiet! I haven't finished with you yet but right now I'm talking to Deke.'

Durango fell silent although his lips moved as if he was mouthing some secret protest.

'Deke! You're not a fool. You must know what's going on by now...'

Cutler nodded gently.

'Pretty obvious. Durango's done some kinda deal with Flash Danton and his bunch to let 'em drive rustled stock across Shoe-string and into those hidden canyons. I know enough about this country to figure out that Shoestring is closest to the Badman's Terri-tory and offers the most cover for anyone wanting to get stolen cattle across the Red River.'

He was staring straight at Spain now and the battered man nodded.

'All right. I had to do something. Told you the drought had given us a beating and I spent a lot of money on that windmill and it's not producing enough water. I'd already been approached by Flash Bill and was considering his offer – hating myself for it, too – when you arrived and told me you wouldn't be getting a pension.' He paused, sighed. 'That did it. I told him OK. He could use the trail across our land and we'd drive our own cows over his tracks so no one could find 'em.'

Deke stared hard at Spain but neither man would lower his gaze.

'I'm supposed to be your pardner, Durango.'

'Yeah, I know, Deke.' Spain glanced at Karen who was now gathering up the bandages and bloody rags she had been using. He frowned and flicked his gaze back and forth between Karen and Deke, trying to give him some silent message.

Cutler didn't know what it was but he forced himself to calm down.

'I don't savvy why you'd do it, specially with a snake like Danton.'

Spain chuckled without mirth.

'You mean my Ranger background and so on? Well, I thought I could point out that Flash was supposed to be dead and that he could be in all kinds of strife if the law found out he was still alive...' His words faded briefly and any suggestion of a smile or banter dropped from him suddenly. 'Know what he said? He said he'd make sure I was in strife, too. But what I should remember was that I wasn't a Ranger any more but I had a wife and a ranch. And way out here, far from law, a lot of bad things could happen to both. If ever he was turned in, he meant. Without his control, he claims the outlaws, and even the Indians, would jump the river and wipe out every settler along it, then run back to the Territory, safe from all but Federal marshals.'

Deke nodded gently.

'And we all know how few of those there are. So, you're saying you had no choice?'

'That's about the size of it.'

'Then how about Salty Shaw and Twist? *You* were supposed to have killed them both down on the Rio–'

'No, you got that wrong. I was *with* the troop that claimed to have nailed those two, but Dal Beattie was commander.'

Spain's gaze was steady on Cutler's face and the latter said nothing for a moment, then nodded.

'Yeah – Dal. He wiped out Red Flats just after Kid McKittrick shot me and died. But I recollect he had a couple of close scrapes with being accused of taking bribes from outlaws down along the Rio.'

'Rangers' own fault for not paying well enough. Yeah, Dal was a mite bent, I reckon. Must've been if that was Salty and Twist you and the nigger nailed. That night on the Rio, when I rode in with my section of the troop, the fight was over. There were dead men everywhere, two of them their own mothers couldn't've recognized. Shotgun work. Dal and a couple of his side-kicks swore it was Salty Shaw and Twist. I had no beef with it. I'm as surprised as you are that they turned up up here still alive.'

'The Red River seems to be a favourite spot for Border hellions to run to,' Deke opined.

'Over in The Nations it does, leastways ... I've thought I recognized one or two from down on the Rio. That's why it was so easy for Flash Danton to get a gang together up here.'

'Breakfast will be ready in a minute.'

Both men looked up, surprised that the kitchen was filled with the aroma of frying bacon and brewing coffee. They had been so intent on their conversation they weren't even aware of Karen preparing the meal.

'Be right there, Karen,' Spain said and

turned a sober gaze on Cutler. 'Well, you satisfied now?'

'Not by a damn sight.'

Durango jumped up. 'What? You calling me a liar?'

'*Durango!*' snapped Karen recognizing the hot anger in her husband's voice. She hefted the heavy skillet by the handle and the warning was plain enough.

Spain sat down slowly, still glaring at Deke.

'I'm not calling you a liar, Durango. I just think you haven't told me everything.'

Spain looked uncomfortable and toyed with his fork.

'Look, you know more than you should right now, I'm doing my best to keep you out of this, Deke. No, don't start griping! *I don't want you mixed up in anything!* That's what it comes down to. I don't like to pull rank but I'm senior partner and what I say goes...' He gave a quick on-off grin, adding: 'For the moment leastways. OK?'

'No, it's not OK. But I know you of old and I guess I'm not going to get any more out of you right now. Just have to say, I'll be keeping my eyes open, wider than usual, from now on.'

Durango's lips tightened and his eyes

flared but he bit back whatever he was going to say as Karen slammed a plate of bacon and eggs in front of him.

'Eat!' she said flatly, hands on hips, her flashing gaze sweeping from one man to the other.

They ate.

Later, sitting on the porch, both stiff and sore, but now sharing a linen bag of Bull Durham mix and Wheatstraw papers as they built cigarettes and lit up, Durango took one deep draw, then exhaled slowly. He looked down at the burning cigarette between his fingers, turning it this way and that.

As Deke exhaled, frowning, Spain said:

'You're gonna be a pain in the butt, I can see that.'

Deke shrugged.

'Told you before – you're my pardner, Durango. You've got troubles, then I want to share 'em with you.'

Spain shook his head in exasperation.

'Knew I damn well taught you too blamed well!' With a jerky motion he took only one more deep draw from the cigarette, then flicked it out into the yard, leaning his arms on the porch rail. He watched a chicken-hawk hovering over Karen's hen-coop, swallows swooping to snatch balls of mud for their nests from the damp spot under the dripping pump, before flying swiftly back into the big barn.

Without turning he said very quietly,

'I tied up with Danton and his bunch because I can make easy money – fast. And I need to make it fast, Deke, for Karen's sake.' He turned slowly, leaning with his elbows on the rail now as he turned haunted eyes to Cutler's rugged face. 'I'm a dying man, Deke. Got maybe six months to live – at most.'

CHAPTER 9

TRACKS

It wasn't until mid-morning, during a session with the blacksmith on the anvil – Deke was determined to pack some muscle back on that wasted arm even if it cost him dearly in pain, and it did – that he thought of something he should have brought up with Durango.

But he was still reeling from Durango's revelation about being a dying man and what should've been an obvious question slipped away and got lost – temporarily at least.

Deke had been truly stunned by the news, was unable to speak for some time. Durango leaned his hips against the porch rail, folded his arms, tapping his fingers against his elbows. His jawline was knotted as he ground his teeth, his eyes lowered, thoughts obviously miles away.

Eventually Cutler stood and went to stand beside him, dropped a hand gently to his shoulder.

'What's the trouble, pard?'

Spain didn't raise his eyes, teeth chewing briefly at his bottom lip.

'Some kind of cancer – in the stomach.'

'Jesus, Durango! Can't they operate or something?'

Spain was shaking his head before Deke had finished speaking.

'Too late. Too far gone.'

'Well, hell almighty! There's got to be something you can do!'

He looked at Deke at last, eyes haunted.

'There is – wait until the pain gets too bad to bear and then...' He slapped his hand against his gun butt.

'Damn! I won't accept that! I mean, even if it got to that stage ... well, there's laudanum. You could take an overdose...' He paused, looking shocked. *'Christ!* What the hell'm I doing! Helping you find a way to kill yourself!'

Spain turned and Deke let his hand drop from his friend's shoulder. They stood looking into each other's faces.

'Deke, when the time comes – no, no, it will, there's nothing can be done about it. It'll come and – well, I might have to call on you to – help me out. I dunno if I could – do – anything to myself...'

Cutler swore, feeling totally helpless.

'Damnit, Durango!' He sighed heavily. ''Course I'd – help – you. But there just has to be something we can do!'

'There's nothing, Deke. Accept it. It took me some time and when I did – well, I thought about Karen. Sorry, old pard, I have to admit I didn't think of you much...'

'Hell, nor d'you need to! No, you've got to make sure Karen's taken care of...' Cutler stiffened. 'That's what's been missing! I couldn't quite accept that you'd deal with these outlaws just to make a quick buck! There had to be a damn good reason for you to do that. Now, of course, I know what it was....'

Spain grabbed him by the forearm, the good one, his fingers digging in, bringing Deke's head up sharply.

'Deke – Karen doesn't know.'

Cutler blinked. 'She – doesn't *know*...? You haven't told her about the cancer?'

'Judas, keep your voice down! No, I haven't. When the pains troubled me I rode down to Dallas on a pretext of looking for a herd of better cattle and saw an Army doctor I know there. You know him, too: Randy Lansing.' Deke nodded: a good man, the only truly caring medic he had ever seen in the Army. The Rangers used his services at times: their funds didn't run to employing a full-time medical officer.

'Well, if Lansing told you there was no hope, I guess I'd have to take his word for it.'

Spain nodded, seeming a little distracted.

'You might've noticed I don't eat chilli like I used to, don't use pepper or Karen's homemade mustard, them sorts of things. You might've even seen me sneaking a glass of cow's milk, for Chris'sake! It's just to help put a lining on the stomach and my gullet, Randy says...' He sobered abruptly. 'But it'll start to spread and I won't be able to keep anything down and then...'

Deke held up a hand. 'By that time, Karen'll *have* to know, Durango.'

Spain nodded jerkily, mouth tight.

'I – might show my yaller streak and kinda – ask you to help out there, Deke, too.'

That shook Cutler some. He didn't fancy having to tell Karen that her husband was dying of cancer and she would soon be a widow. But – that was the kind of chore pardners did for each other.... He offered his hand and Spain gripped firmly.

'I sure won't enjoy it, but – I'll do whatever you want, Durango.'

Spain grinned widely, clasped Deke's

hand in both of his. *'Gracias, amigo, muchas gracias!* Let's hope it's a long time off, huh...?'

'A *damn* long time,' Deke said fervently.

It was something he couldn't shake, even while he was making new shoes for the grey and the blacksmith was showing him how to twist red-hot bar-iron into fancy designs for fireplace and wall ornaments, candlesticks and firetongs. Deke wondered how *he* would take the news that he had incurable cancer of the stomach well, at least he wouldn't have any wife or family to worry about. It must be sheer hell for Spain to live with that kind of secret.

He savvied now why the man had thrown out all his ethics: Deke would likely have done the same if he had had Karen for a wife – or any wife. Bending the law a little, even a lot, didn't matter a damn under such circumstances. There was no other way that she could survive after Spain died: this was a quick way to get some money for her, enough, anyway, to see her through the funeral and maybe pay off the debts so she wouldn't have to sell Shoestring. Deke sure wouldn't stand in her way. Or, maybe she would be glad to get rid of it.

Then what? Maybe she would go back to Denver and her family, start to live how she used to before she married Durango.

Maybe she would be glad of any help he could offer. Maybe whatever might have been between them once would have a chance to blossom and...

'Hey, Deke! What you makin', man? A goddamn broadsword...?'

The smith's rough voice startled Deke out of his thoughts and he saw that instead of just adding a barley sugar twist to the squared bar-iron he had been forging, he had hammered it out into the semblance of a knife blade, or even the beginning of a broadsword or spear point...

'Sorry, Mitch. Daydreaming.'

'Ah, it don't matter. Can always turn it into a knife, wrap rawhide round the tang and sell it to Ringo for an Injun blade – he's dumb enough to believe it, bein' kinda partial to knives.'

Deke was only half-listening. He could have kicked himself: where did he get off even thinking about Karen in that way when Durango would have to die before anything in that line even began...?

You're a lousy, two-timing son of a bitch, Deacon Cutler! Durango don't deserve a

*conniving pardner like you – and you sure as
hell don't deserve him! Now take a hitch in that
hackamore and rein down, you hear? You've got
a ranch to run, you and Durango...*

Cutler and Jimmy Taggart went out to gather
in some mustangs, which the wrangler
would break in enough to work brush cattle.
They rode up into ridge country above the
river and Jimmy surprised Deke with his
knowledge of horses.

'Grew up in Wyomin',' the kid explained
when they stopped for a smoke on a
projecting rocky ledge. The river wound
away into the mysterious land to the north,
though Deke knew the 'mystery' part was all
in a man's mind: it looked little different
from any other part of the country around
here except maybe it was a little greener and
the timber was a little thicker. Still, there
were arid sections, too, which would make
the Staked Plains look like a public garden.

'My old man never had much, no
education, used his fists to settle most
arguments, his gun once or twice. But he
knew hosses. Folk rode in from three States
away for his advice.' He grinned sheepishly.
'Anyway, he taught me plenty and I guess
it's took, because I reckon I get along better

with hosses than I do with people at times.'

Deke smiled.

'Plenty of times I prefer old Grey's company to other folk, too, kid. You gonna be a wrangler all your life?'

'Not if I can help it – want my own hoss ranch eventually. Meantime, thought I might try some rodeo work after I leave here. Lot of money to be made there.' He paused as if making some sort of decision about Cutler, then said, quietly: 'If you don't mind losin' once in a while.'

Deke frowned.

'You mean, throw a ride, just like throwing a prize fight?'

Jimmy flushed but nodded eagerly enough.

'Yeah. Wouldn't hurt now and again. Earn some quick money to get my spread.'

'Well, you could lose one reputation – as a top rider – and gain another – as a man who doesn't mind selling out.'

Taggart paled, mouth tightening.

'I don't see it that way!'

'Well, most other folk would. 'Course, if you don't care a damn about what folk think of you, you might last a couple years on the rodeo circuit – before you find you can't get a decent job anywhere because no one'll trust you.'

'Aw! It don't work like that. Anyways, how about you and Durango? You two're doin' deals with them outlaws across the river.'

Deke butted out his cigarette stub against the saddle horn before dropping it to the ground.

'Kid, you could be right. But Durango has a real solid reason for making those deals.'

'I would have, too – to make a fast buck!'

'Your Old Man teach you that it was OK to sell out like that?'

'No-o. But I kinda picked up on it after he died and I took off and seen how most men made extra *dinero*.'

'You get your share now, don't you?' Deke asked softly.

Jimmy tossed his head.

'Few dollars, sure, just for lookin' the other way. But I ain't in a position to earn real money, like Ringo and Hal Tripp and Jno. They can use their guns...'

'How many others in the crew are in this deal?'

Jimmy frowned deeper.

'You'd best ask Durango. C'mon, if we're gonna catch them broncs down at the waterhole ...'

The kid wheeled away and Deke smiled to himself as he followed slowly; Jimmy was either pretty loyal or just plain dumb.

Either way, he could get himself into a lot of trouble.

They were bringing down a bunch of wild-eyed, mane-flying Mustangs in the afternoon, following a narrow, ragged trail through a series of dry washes that Deke hadn't seen before. But the kid knew that trail and it was narrow and twisting enough to keep the still wild horses in Indian file. The kid told Cutler that it ended in a small blind draw which would hold the horses overnight. He had already prepared sliding rails that could be pulled swiftly into place after the last animal thundered in.

It worked well and then, after making sure the rails were all tight in their niches, they turned to walk back to their mounts.

'Judas goddamn priest!' exclaimed Jimmy Taggart.

It was such an exclamation of surprise that Deke started to draw his six-gun even as he turned. Then he froze.

The Samburu was standing there, only three yards away, his red robe bright against the drab earth-colour of the dry wash, the blade of his long spear flashing in the westering sun. Jimmy glanced quickly at Deke.

'What's he want?'

'Guess we'll have to ask. Howdy, Sam.' Deke had an urge to lift a hand, palm out, the way whitemen greeted Indians but something told him that it wasn't appropriate here. 'Dutch Pete around?' he asked instead.

The Samburu warrior, he noted now, was wearing what he thought was a wig, a huge mass of russet-coloured coarse hair, swept back, adding at least a foot to his height, held in place with a band that had been worked with strange angular designs and some beads. Later, he learned that the 'wig' was the mane of a lion.

'Sam has earned the right to wear it,' Dutch Pete told him when they met up on the slopes overlooking the sharp bend of the Red River within spitting distance of outlaw territory. 'Like the Masai, a tribe they're distantly related to, the Samburu warriors prove themselves by hunting lions on foot, armed only with a single spear. No knife, no *panga*.'

But, right now, Deke didn't know this, although he thought the mane gave the tall, skinny warrior much more dignity and pride.

'Come,' Sam said, pointing his spear at Cutler.

'Hey, watch that thing!' cried Jimmy, dodging partly behind Cutler.

'Where, Sam?'

'Come,' the Samburu repeated and this time he pointed up the mountain with his spear hand.

'Pete wants to see me?' Deke asked and Sam nodded. 'OK. Jimmy, I'll see you back at Shoestring.'

'You ain't goin' with him!'

'He's friendly. Saved my life a while back when he speared that outlaw, Salty Shaw. He's not about to cut my throat now.'

Jimmy wasn't any too sure about that but he nodded and watched as Deke mounted. The Samburu turned silently and began striding up the steep slope as easily as he would walk across a room. Deke waved briefly and set the horse after him.

When Dutch Pete stepped out from behind some rocks on a high bench, a little later, Sam simply disappeared. Deke knew the man wouldn't be far away but he hadn't seen where he went.

Pete shook hands with Cutler.

'Saw you and the kid catching the wild horses. He's pretty good.'

'Yeah. Haven't seen you around for a few days.'

'Still looking for bear tracks. I've found some but I think they're a couple days old. And I don't know if it's a grizzly or a brown or black. You seemed to know just by looking at the tracks that other time, so I sent Sam down. Can you spare me a little time?'

Deke glanced at the assegai that Van Rensberg held.

'I dunno as I'd want it on my conscience, putting you on to a bear with only that thing as a weapon.'

Dutch Pete grinned, brandishing the short spear.

'My favourite weapon. This blade has drunk a lot of blood over the years – lion, leopard, kudu, buffalo, rhino, crocodile – it thirsts for the most feared animal on this continent and that surely must be the grizzly.' Pete clapped a heavy arm about Deke's shoulders. 'Humour me, Deke. Ah! I see you didn't wince then! Your health has improved, eh, man?'

'Some. Hope to keep it that way or make it even better. Chasing a bear in these hills wasn't exactly what I had in mind.'

'Never know just how it could pay off,' the South African said enigmatically and when Deke looked at him quizzically he only winked. 'Like I said, man – humour me, eh?

Who knows what we might find.'

'Where're the tracks?'

'Up and over the crest. Might've even crossed the river,' Pete said, winking. 'Let's take a look.'

There was something more to this than just a chance meeting in the wilderness, Cutler decided. And he wished he knew where the Samburu had got to go.

The tracks led down to the river but Deke doubted the bear had crossed: the water was too deep. Deke explained the difference between a black bear – which was the most likely quarry – and a grizzly, not usual in this country.

'A black'll rip your head off just as quickly as a grizz, Pete. But he's smaller as a rule, not so easy to rile, and his footprints are distinctive.' He squatted beside some fairly large prints, not all that distinct in the mud or further along the bank in looser soil. 'A grizzly's claws are hardly ever less than two inches long. But a black's are no more than an inch and a half. The toes are the giveaway. The grizzly's toes on the front feet are in a near-straight line. But a black's have a definite curve – like these here. The hind foot on a black has a wedge in the instep too, and a rounded heel, but the grizzly has no instep and the heel is pointed. There'll be other sign, too.'

Deke stood, arms akimbo and looked around. He pointed to a pine tree.

'There. Bears like to rub against pines and they take the bark off. Higher up and here, down at the bottom, he's torn strips of bark off to get at the syrupy sap. There's a little blood here.'

'Not too badly hurt to fight, I hope!'

'You'll get your fight, Pete, if you ever catch up with him. See that deadfall yonder? All smashed up. He did that, looking for ants in the rotting wood. Hurt or not, he's still got plenty of strength left.'

'Big?'

'That I can't say for sure but I'd guess maybe three hundred pounds. Did you see him at all?'

Pete shook his head and turned to the silent Samburu, who had now reappeared, and spoke rapidly in some strange language. Sam squatted, and with a slim ebony finger drew an outline of a bear in the sandy soil. Deke studied it briefly.

'If this is accurate–'

'It will be. Sam's got a hawk's eyes.'

'OK. See? No hunched shoulders? No hump or dished-in face profile – both of which are characteristics of a grizzly. This is definitely a black – straight-face profile, no long-haired ruff...'

They followed the tracks up the slope and across the face and Deke began to recognize landmarks. He suddenly turned to van Rensberg.

'What's your game, Pete?'

Dutch Pete blinked his puzzlement. 'Game?'

'Yeah. We didn't come quite this far the other day but I'll bet my eye teeth these are the same tracks we saw then. We're following that same bear who was favouring his right hind foot. So why the hell have you brought me up here when you knew all along the bear who made those tracks was long gone?'

'Well, I needed help to look for some...'

Before Pete could continue, the Samburu let out a wild cry from up the timbered slope. They jerked around – to see a red-eyed, slavering bear lumbering out of the bushes above, raging after the running warrior, coming at them all like the lead boulder in an avalanche.

CHAPTER 10

RED RIVER BATTLE

Dutch Pete van Rensberg gave a crazy-sounding war cry and leapt to his feet, assegai in both hands. Still yelling he ran to meet the bear while the Samburu veered sharply, robe flying behind, lion-mane wafting in the wind of his passage, skidding as he almost fell.

Deke Cutler slipped in getting to his feet, too, and then whipped out his six-gun, wishing he had his rifle. But there was a *clang* and his wrist jarred as Sam's spear-blade knocked the pistol from his hand. He shook his head at Deke, the lion-mane jerking from side to side. There were beads of sweat on his black face as he pointed to Dutch Pete.

The man had confronted the bear, eager for the battle, crouching, assegai thrusting several times. The animal had given van Rensberg his full attention now, slapped at the long blade of the spear. It cut the paw and he gave a strangely feminine yelp as he withdrew his leg quickly. Van Rensberg's rugged face was aglow with excitement. He hunched down, wide shoulders knotted with tension, his free hand out to one side as a kind of balance to the right arm which held the short spear about midway along the shaft. The bear was limping and as it turned upslope – where Pete had worked so that he was slightly above the animal – Deke saw the cloud of flies and yellow pus in a long shallow bullet-wound in the right haunch. This would have accounted for the limp that had showed up in the lie of his tracks. Someone had taken a shot at him, winged him, but thought better of chasing after the animal to finish it off. He had likely gone to ground to literally lick his wounds, been disturbed by the trackers.

Now he was no doubt feeling plenty of pain from the infected wound and he was every bit as dangerous and killing-mad as an enraged grizzly twice his size.

'It's suicidal, Pete!' Cutler yelled, scooping up his Colt. The Samburu looked narrowly at him, long spear raised, and Deke was suddenly aware that the warrior was prepared to kill him in order to give van Rensberg his wish of fighting a bear with only the assegai.

'He's gonna get killed!' Deke told Sam angrily. 'The damn fool doesn't savvy what bears are like when they're good and mad! They can be worse than any goddamn lion, I'll bet!'

Sam's dark eyes were unwavering, as was the spearpoint. It was lined up on the centre of Deke's chest.

'You're both plumb loco!' Cutler snapped, shaking his head slowly as he watched Dutch Pete dodge and thrust. *He's getting ready to lunge!'* he yelled warningly.

Van Rensberg had fought enough animals in this manner to recognize the attack attitudes of the bear's body. He jumped down the slope as the bear hurled itself at the place where he had been a moment earlier, claws raking. But they only raked air and then the animal squealed like a pig as the assegai blade sank half its length into his side. Blood spurted and the bear clawed at the sharp metal that was tormenting it. Pete staggered as the claws struck the withdrawing blade and almost tore the weapon from his grasp. He slipped and slid down the slope. In a blurred movement, faster than the blink of an eye, the wounded bear jumped and landed partly on van Rensberg, knocking him sprawling. The big South

African grunted, recovered, but his spear arm swung wide.

The weapon fell from opening fingers but Pete closed them swiftly, just managing to wrap them around the end of the shaft as the bear's claws ripped through his shirt – and his flesh. He roared in pain as blood flowed, going down to one knee, and the bear stomped down, making its own snarling, roaring, chest-deep sounds. It swiped with a foreleg and van Rensberg, fighting to get up, was struck on the right shoulder. The force of the blow hurled him, spinning, across the face of the slope. He fell awkwardly and lost his grip on the assegai.

Deke Cutler was astonished to see the Samburu throw himself between the bear and the injured van Rensberg, jabbing with his own spear, but only in weak, short strokes so that the razor-sharp blade barely penetrated the black bear's skin beneath the matted hair of coat: irritating but not deeply wounding. He was giving Dutch Pete every chance to make his kill...

Cutler shook his head slowly, hardly believing what he was seeing.

The thrusts must have been deep enough to hurt, for the bear reared and stumbled as it swiped at the tall black man. Claws caught in the red robe and tore it half off the lean ebony body. Sam had his panga slung on a strip of rhino-hide around his narrow waist but made no attempt to use it, even as slavering jaws reached for him.

Deke thought, *To hell with this!* and raised his six-gun. But even as more claws ripped the Samburu across the ribs, exposing the whiteness of bone, he swung the long-handled spear and Deke was forced to duck and jump back. By the time he had righted himself, Dutch Pete had made his move.

With the Samburu writhing and screaming now as the bear's fangs sank into his skinny left shoulder, spear flailing wildly but ineffectually, van Rensberg, bleeding and cut badly, too, thrust the assegai deep under the arch of the bear's ribs. The animal bellowed, rearing, beating and tearing at the short shaft. Dutch Pete, crouched, twisted, teeth bared, withdrew the blade and as the bear staggered and made to slash with a wicked set of scything claws, stabbed deep again, throwing all his weight on to the spear.

It sank completely into the bear and the jerking, writhing animal hurled Pete down the slope so that his tumbling body knocked Cutler off his feet. The bear ripped and tore at the bloody shaft. Wood splintered. The animal took a single staggering step down-hill, tried to stay balanced but lost out and fell with a crash that Deke later swore shook the whole damn mountain.

He dragged the bloody and barely conscious van Rensberg out of the way, seeing Sam's frail-looking body jerking loosely as the bear rolled over him. The animal, amazingly, climbed to its feet, started to run in wild, widening circles, trying to withdraw the splintered shaft and blade. Blood was everywhere, drenching the matted coat, spewing from the chomping jaws, until the bear dropped to its knees and toppled on to its side, snorting, jerking as it tried to get up, until, finally, its great broody head flopped loosely on the neck and with one final belching exhalation, it died.

Deke did what he could for the two men from Africa – and it was little enough. They were both slashed and cut deeply, though the Samburu was in the worse condition by far. He was conscious but didn't make a sound, his eye-whites now yellow, the dark pupils staring but seeing something far from this Red River hillside. Deke tore up his robe into strips.

'Sam? Is he – OK?' grated van Rensberg, biting back on the surges of pain that wracked his body.

'No. He'll die if we don't get him to a doctor. You're not in very good shape yourself.'

'I'm ... fine.' Dutch Pete strained and struggled until he could see the bear's body. He grinned through bloody lips. 'I – did – it...'

'Thanks to Sam. He damn near died for you. May yet.'

Van Rensberg nodded solemnly. 'Faithful unto death.' But there was no levity in his quote. 'A fine – warrior.'

'A fine *man*,'Deke corrected him. 'I'll have to get help from Shoestring.'

'No – wait. There's an army patrol out of Fort Montague – camped at the Salt Fork, just downstream a'ways. There'll be a – medic there...'

'How do you know about the army camp?'

'Saw it. Leave me here with – Sam. The doctor'll come...'

'I wouldn't bet on it. Army doctors ain't always obliging. Maybe I better get a buckboard from Shoestring.'

'Eh, man! *He'll come!* Now get a move on, eh? Sam's dying! *Go!*'

Deke hesitated only briefly and then left all the rags he could – having torn up his spare shirts and neckerchiefs in an effort to bind the terrible wounds – and his water bottle and rifle. Not that either man was fit enough to shoot but it seemed a likely precaution to take.

Then he hurried to the grey, glanced at the westering sun, and spurred away to the east, towards the Salt Fork, hoping van Rensberg knew what he was talking about.

It wasn't unusual for the army to patrol the Red River, but it was unusual for them to be this far up. In the past they had stuck mainly to the downstream areas, on the Texas side, in a show of power, but it seemed strange to him that Dutch Pete of all people should know the location of a soldiers' camp when local settlers weren't aware of it.

The soldiers were right where Dutch Pete said they would be – camped on the Salt Fork of the Red. But not where just anyone could see them.

Cutler reined down at first, knowing he was nearing the river junction, looking around for some sign of the army. There was movement in the timber and a soldier rode out on a long-legged black, his Trapdoor Springfield rifle across his thighs. Deke noted that the big hammer was already cocked.

This man was a corporal, a little older than

Deke and chewing tobacco. He nodded then spat a brown stream to his left.

'Howdy. Lookin' for somethin' – or someone?'

Cutler reined down, hipping slightly to the left so he could reach his six-gun fast if he needed to: an old precaution that had helped keep him alive through his Texas Ranger years.

'Looking for your commanding officer, matter of fact, corp.'

'Oh? Who would that be now?'

'You'd know better' n me, I guess. It's urgent. There're two men tore up by a bear upstream about three miles, a little less, I believe you've a medic with you.'

The corporal looked all round and spat another tream, shrugging.

'You see anyone else?'

'C'mon, forget the delays! I need that doctor.' Cutler moved on the last word and the soldier's rifle was only barely lifted off his thighs when he gaped, staring down the muzzle of Deke's cocked six-shooter.

'Hell al-doubledamn-mighty! How'd you do that?'

'The sawbones, goddamnit! Those men are bleeding to death!'

Cutler reached across and yanked the rifle

from the man's hands, uncocking the weapon. The corporal's face tightened and he looked suddenly worried.

'Hey! I'm in trouble if the lieutenant knows you took my gun off me.'

'Climb down, corp – and do it slow and easy.'

The soldier didn't like taking orders but he complied. And while he was easing down in the stirrup, Cutler unloaded the Springfield, pocketed the big shell and tossed the gun across.

'Lieutenant doesn't need to know. But you lead me in or he'll know when he hears the shot.'

The corporal frowned and climbed back into his saddle.

'What shot?'

'When I shoot you in the leg.'

There was no more delay. The soldier led Cutler through the timber and along a winding trail through a thicket, then into a draw where a company of soldiers were camped. Lieutenant Craig was young and when he heard Cutler's name he stiffened.

'*Deke* Cutler? Texas Rangers?'

'Not any longer. Running the Shoestring spread with another ex-Ranger, Durango Spain.'

Craig nodded soberly. 'Of course – and who are these men who were attacked by a bear?'

Deke told him and the man was suddenly galvanized, snapping at the corporal:

'Fetch Doc Lansing! Tell him to bring a full medical kit – and detail four men to escort us to the injured. It's Dutch Pete and Long Sam!'

Cutler was surprised at the sudden burst of efficiency amongst the lounging soldiers – Dutch Pete's name seemed to mean something here. They were on the trail upstream in fifteen minutes.

It was a gory job, treating the injured, but Cutler rolled up his sleeves and helped the doctor cleanse and sew the terrible wounds on van Rensberg and the unconscious Samburu warrior. Lansing showed no surprise at seeing them and Deke had a notion that he already knew both men.

There was something strange going on here, he allowed to himself. Mighty strange....

There had been no time wasted getting here and Cutler had had little chance to speak with Doctor Randy Lansing. Helping the medic, their verbal exchanges had been limited to brief commands, asking for the iodine, or fresh sutures.

The escort soldiers stood around marvelling at the bear's carcass with the broken spear still protruding.

It was getting dark by the time the doctor sat back on his hams, mopping sweat from his face with a soiled rag.

'They gonna make it, doc?' Deke asked.

Lansing pursed his lips, looked from one to the other of the wounded men now swathed in bandages, sleeping from heavy doses of laudanum.

'Dutch Pete'll be all right, quite heavily scarred, but I guess he won't mind that. The Samburu...? Well, I don't know. If he was a white man he'd be dead already. But just look at the build of him! Skin and leather and bone. Nothing to him. Yet he has a fighting spirit stronger than any I've come across – and I've doctored Apaches, Comanches and Sioux, whose warriors are certainly not noted for their fraility. It's amazing, but I suppose he led a hard life in the Dark Continent.'

Cutler looked steadily into Lansing's weary face.

'You know Pete and Sam before this, doc?'

'Why do you ask?'

'C'mon, doc! This is Deke Cutler, remember? Don't answer my questions by asking another! We've had too many drinks in the sutler's bar for that!'

Lansing sighed.

'You're right, of course, Deke. But I can't say anything. It's up to the lieutenant, I guess.'

'There's some mystery here, Doc. Pete got me up here on a pretext of tracking down a wounded bear – one we'd found sign of – days earlier...'

'Well, you certainly succeeded in flushing him out this time.'

'Don't try to get off the subject, Doc. Pete was as surprised as I was when the bear attacked: neither of us expected to find it so close.'

Lansing remained silent, started to pack a pipe. Cutler shook his head slowly.

'Well, OK. There's something going on I don't know about and you don't want to tell me. Maybe you can tell me how come a sawbones as good as you, one who's just sewed together a couple of men I'd've said I'd be burying before sundown, can't do more for Durango Spain.'

Doc was just lighting his pipe, covering the bowl with the vesta box to make it draw. He looked up slowly, puzzled, as smoke wreathed around his head.

'What would you expect me to do for Durango?'

'Well, I've said for years you're one helluva fine doctor, and you try to keep up with the latest medical methods. Why can't you operate on Durango?'

Lansing was really frowning now, allowing his pipe to go out as he stared at Deke Cutler. 'Now why would I want to operate on Durango?'

'Well, I guess you don't, but surely it's worth a try, even if it's only to see just how bad the cancer is.'

Randy Lansing stiffened and stood slowly.

'Cancer? Deke, what the *hell* are you talking about?'

Cutler's belly was knotted tightly now and he felt the stinging behind his eyes that always came when he had to face danger – or hear something he knew in advance he wasn't going to like.

'Durango's dying of cancer. You told him he has only six months to live at most,' he said slowly, quietly, and very distinctly.

Lansing held his gaze rock-steady.

'Deke, I haven't seen Durango in almost a year. I know nothing about any cancer, or, in fact, anything at all about his present state of health. But the last time I saw him, he was fitter than you or me. And I'd be surprised if he died this side of seventy – or even later.'

CHAPTER 11

TRUTH AND CONSEQUENCES

It was the middle of the morning when Deke Cutler rode the weary grey into the Shoestring ranchyard. Karen was on the porch; she jumped up out of her cane chair when she saw him and ran down towards the corrals.

He was unsaddling when she came up, looking anxious.

'Oh, Deke! Where've you been? We've been worried about you. Jimmy told us that tall black man of Dutch Pete's took you off somewhere and we sent men out looking when you hadn't come in by dark. They found a dead bear with a spear in it and...'

He took her by the shoulders, looking down into her face, smiling faintly.

'Take it easy. I'm all right. Dutch Pete killed the bear...'

'Yes, we surmised that. But the men said there was – blood everywhere...'

'Mostly the bear's, but considerable

belonging to Pete and Sam.' Deke glanced up when Durango came across from the barn where he had apparently been working with a wood plane for curled shavings were adhering to his trousers. He looked pretty grim.

'The hell've you been, Deke?' He sounded as annoyed as he looked. 'I've had men out on the river half the damn night looking for you.'

'I could use a cup of coffee,' Cutler said, nodding towards the house. 'I'll tell you all about it then, OK?'

'Of course,' Karen said, turning and starting away. 'You get washed up and I'll make you a meal.'

'Just coffee thanks. I've eaten.'

Durango waited until she was entering the house, then asked:

'Where'd you eat in that country?'

'Not there. In town. I had to get Pete and that Samburu to a medic. Borrowed a couple of horses from Dutch Pete's spread and made two travois.'

They started slowly towards the house. If Spain thought Deke was lying he hid it pretty well.

'Lots of tracks up around that bear, Deke. Shod horses. More than the three which

161

would've been your grey and the two horses you borrowed.'

'Some of Pete's men rode back with me.'

Durango nodded thoughtfully.

'OK. How come you went with Pete's nigger when you was s'posed to be helping Jimmy Taggart with the mustangs?'

'They were corralled. Jimmy aimed to let 'em settle overnight before he started in to break 'em.'

They were at the washbench now and Deke propped his battered rifle against it, stripped to the waist and pumped water into a tin bowl. As he washed, Durango casually examined the rifle. When he picked it up, Deke's shirt fell off the bench, caught briefly in the foresight. Durango stooped for it and something that glittered fell out of the pocket. He retrieved it and slowly stood as Deke shook water from his hair and, eyes closed, groped for the rag of towel hanging on a nail. Durango let him grope, studied the .45/.70 calibre cartridge, hefting it, turning it this way and that, lips pursed thoughtfully. He started to speak, then changed his mind and dropped the cartridge into his pocket as Deke located the towel and wiped water from his eyes, opened them and blinked.

He nodded to the torn, filthy, blood-spattered shirt in Durango's hand.

'Got a shirt I can borrow? I tore up my spares to bandage Pete and Sam.'

'Yeah. There'll be one inside. Let's go get that coffee and hear your story.'

Cutler made it brief, not mentioning the army patrol or Doc Lansing – or that he had ridden back to the fort with Lieutenant Craig to see Captain Bannister before returning to Shoestring.

'They're both in the Wichita Falls infirmary now. Pete will make it OK but I'm not sure about the Samburu.'

'He must be very ... loyal,' Karen opined. 'I mean, to throw himself between a crazy bear and Pete van Rensberg. It's more than loyalty, isn't it? It's – love, I suppose.'

'They grew up together in Kenya, so Pete said. If you can use "love" for how one man feels about another, I guess that's what it must be.'

Spain snorted, set down his coffee cup.

'Well, I'd appreciate your getting word back to me if anything else like that happens, Deke. Can't have the men wasting time looking for you when you're OK.'

'There was no time to let you know, Durango,' Deke told him soberly, watching the man's face. 'And I doubt there'll ever be another occasion like that one. Unless you know someone else who's crazy enough to want to fight a bear hand-to-hand...?'

Spain smiled crookedly.

'Reckon they're few and far between. OK, well, you want to go back out and help Jimmy with the mustangs? Jno's with him but I've got another job I'd rather put him on.'

Karen looked sharply at her husband and then at Cutler.

'Deke looks all done-in, Durango...'

Spain arched his eyebrows.

'Yeah? You want to take a rest, pard?' There was a slight emphasis on the 'pard' and Deke knew Spain was reminding him he was supposed to be a working partner.

'I'll go help Jimmy.'

'Send Jno back. Tell him I've got an urgent job for him.'

'Maybe I could do it, save the time riding out to where Jimmy is and–'

'No. I want Jno for this. Just send him in.'

Durango walked out into the yard. Deke finished his coffee and rose to his feet, Karen's eye on him.

'Good coffee, Karen. Thanks.'

'Deke. Is there something ... wrong between you and Durango? You both seem

... strained, and with more meaning when you speak to each other than is apparent to an outsider.'

Cutler shrugged.

'I'm tired and it was no fun helping Randy Lansing sew up Pete and Sam...'

Her eyes widened.

'You ... *helped?*'

'It had to be done quickly. They'd both lost heaps of blood.' He moved his gaze away from her face and she frowned slightly. 'I'd better be getting back to young Jimmy.'

She watched him go, thoughtfully, somehow disappointed but she wasn't quite sure why. She was still frowning when she waved him off ten minutes later as he rode out on a chestnut mare.

Big Jno was leaning on the rails, watching Taggart work one of the mustangs when Deke rode in and dismounted. He turned his head slowly, looking at the tall Texan over his left shoulder. Then he turned back to watch Taggart without speaking.

'Durango wants you back at the ranch.'

Jno grunted, not moving.

'He says it's urgent.'

'Yeah?' Jno still didn't look at him.

Deke hesitated, then said; 'Well, you can

explain to him when you finally decide to amble in.'

'I'll do that.' Jno turned to look at him now, leaning back against the rails. Jimmy had seen him, too, left the horse he was working tethered to the snubbing post in the clearing, a sack across its eyes. It stood there, quivering.

Deke stiffened.

'What happened to your face?' he asked Jimmy.

Taggart touched his puffy, bruised eyes and the two deep cuts to his mouth. He glanced at Jno.

'Hoss threw him and he kissed the ground,' the big man said. 'Well, I better be goin', I guess.'

As the man roughly shouldered past, Deke grabbed him by a thick arm, swinging him around and pushing him back against the rails. Jimmy gasped.

'Deke. It's all right! It ... happened like Jno said.'

Cutler didn't take his eyes off Jno.

'I recognize fist marks when I see them. You been beating-up on Jimmy. Why?'

'You reckon you know fist marks, huh? See if you recognize this one!'

It came fast and unexpectedly low. Deke

gagged and stepped back fast, one leg wobbling, as his breath was cut. Jimmy yelled and tried to hold Jno back but the big man swung an arm and sent the kid rolling in the dust. He planted his thick legs wide and knocked Deke's hat off, twisting his fingers in the long hair. He bared his teeth in a sneer as he almost lazily yanked Deke's head up and drove a punch into his face. Deke, still fighting for a breath, managed to turn his head slightly and the blow skidded along his jaw. But he saw a Fourth of July in the bright mountain sunshine and his ears rang.

Jno swore because his blow hadn't landed squarely and drew his arm back for a second try. Deke brought a hand up into his crotch and twisted savagely. Jno made a sick yelping, half-retching sound and his legs sagged as he doubled over, releasing Deke. Cutler lifted a knee into his face, held him there, gave him another knee in the same place. He felt nose cartilage crunch and blood sprayed over his trousers. Jno stumbled into the rails and Deke went after him, arms hammering like pistons, working over the man's sweaty body from waistline to throat.

Jno dropped to his knees, head lolling on his shoulders, face bloody, nose mashed back twice as wide as originally. His eyes were crossed and Deke took a handful of the greasy black curls and smashed his forehead into the rails. Jno groaned and flopped down, one arm hooking through the bottom rail, all that stopped him from falling completely.

Breathing hard, shaking his right hand because it hurt after connecting with Jno's jaw so many times, Cutler looked at Jimmy and wiped some blood and sweat off his face.

'Why'd – he – beat – you – kid?'

Jimmy swallowed, obviously glad to see Jno beaten but, at the same time, a little afraid – no doubt wondering how the bully would exact his vengeance upon him when Deke wasn't around.

'He – he wanted to know if it looked like you'd arranged for that skinny nigger to come get you and take you to see Dutch Pete. I told him I din' know but he kept at me, in the end...' he licked his split lips, 'I – told him you – you'd said you might be meetin' someone. I'm sorry, Deke, but I thought he was gonna – kill me.'

Deke touched the boy's shoulder. 'It's OK, Jimmy – no harm done. Now, we'd better get to that bronc you've got tied to the snubbing post before he pulls it out of the ground.'

'What about – him?' Jimmy gestured to the barely stirring Jno.

'He'll ride out when he comes round.'

Deke leaned down, took Jno's six-gun and then went to the battered man's horse and removed the rifle from the saddle scabbard. He and Jimmy helped Jno, still punchy, dazed, into his saddle and Deke led the horse out of the draw, slapped his hat across its rump and set it on the trail back to Shoestring headquarters, Jno swaying as if drunk.

Spain had no sympathy for Jno as the man washed up at the bench and had Ringo, recovering from his earlier gunshot wound, set his nose. It was rough and painful and Jno yelled and cussed-out Ringo so bad the man simply said: 'Do the damn thing yourself!' and walked back into the bunkhouse.

Spain stared coldly at Jno as he held his mashed nose gently, moaning, but getting so sign of compassion.

'You were a fool to beat the kid. He's dumb, does what he's told, but he doesn't know anything more than what I want him to.'

'He said Cutler was lookin' to meet some-one.'

'Aah. After ten minutes of you beating on him, he'd say anything.' Spain glanced around, making sure none of the other hands was near, and took the big cartridge from his pocket. 'Found this in Deke's shirt.'

Jno looked up sharply and winced because of it. 'Hell, that's army! Trapdoor Springfield.'

Spain nodded.

'You seen any sign of army patrols lately?'

'Hell no! I'd've told you right away, Durango. But – all them hoofmarks I found near the dead bear...'

'He says it was men from the Assegai spread.'

Jno thought about it.

'Mebbe – but come to think of it, the boot marks'd be more like army than cowhands.'

Durango Spain's mouth tightened and his eyes narrowed. 'Goddamn! I suspected Deke right from the word go. Aw, he'd been bad-hurt, no question, but there was just ... something... Hell, I taught him all he knows.' He laughed shortly. 'Christ, I hammered it into him how a Ranger was s'posed to act, where his loyalties lay, that he *never* stopped being a Ranger, even after he left the Service.'

'Got yourself to blame then,' Jno grated

with a certain amount of satisfaction, although he cringed slightly at the look Spain threw in his direction.

'I like Deke. Man always has a soft spot for his protégé, I guess – but... The time's come to haul rein right now. Can't afford any loose ends at this stage.' He smiled thinly at the battered, unhappy man before him. 'Jno, I think I need you to do a special job for me. Worth an extra fifty?'

Although it hurt like hell, Jno smiled.

'You bet!'

Jimmy Taggart was a good bronc-buster. He had patience which was the key to the whole thing, but apart from that there seemed to be a definite affinity with horses. No, not just horses, with *animals* in general.

There were squirrels and lizards and several birds scavenging around their camp and Jimmy always had some titbits ready when they appeared. In no time at all, he had these dwellers of the woods taking food out of his hands, sitting within a yard of him and eating it, waiting for more.

With the horses, well, they gave him quite a few wild buckjumps and sunfishing, biting, rolls, and lots of snorting and straight-legging that made Cutler wince just watching:

he could *feel* the jolt clear through his spine and up into his skull even while he was sitting on the rails, smoking, and Jimmy was being hurled to hell and back.

But the kid didn't seem to mind. He was weary and aching and a couple of times, after being sent flying out of the saddle, he was hurt, limping around some, but he was philosophical about it.

'Goes with the job,' he said, holding a dirty cloth to a bleeding nose, his teeth chipped. 'They don't aim to hurt me – just make a game out of it.'

So Cutler came to admire the youngster and over supper he asked quietly:

'Jimmy, while you've been searching for mustangs – you notice anything out of the ordinary around the hills? This side of the river or over in the Nations. I take it you go across sometimes?'

Jimmy Taggart looked a mite uncomfortable.

'Sure. But usually I have Jno or Hal with me. They leave me to look for mustangs while they go off somewhere. Hey! You know the word mustang comes from the Spanish *mestero*? Meaning "stray"...'

'Yeah, Jim, I know that. Don't try to change the subject, kid. This is important: have you seen anything ... strange?'

'Like what?' Taggart asked, a little sullen and plainly worried now.

'Well, you know where Jno and Hal Tripp go to? If they meet someone, maybe...?'

Jimmy squirmed.

'I ain't s'posed to talk about this stuff, Deke.'

Cutler nodded.

'I know Durango would've warned you, but...'

Taggart shook his head.

'No, not Durango. Hal Tripp and Jno. They told half a dozen of us if we ever spoke of ... things we saw we'd end up with a bullet in the head instead of a few extra bucks in the pay packet.'

'Sounds like someone's got something to hide.'

Jimmy poked at the fire, spilled coffee as he made to refill his cup. He didn't look at Deke.

'You still a Ranger? That's what everyone thinks, you know.'

'Well, they're wrong, Jimmy. I quit the Rangers and came here to run the ranch with Durango as my pardner. But there seems to be a lot going on that I don't know about. I thought Spain had some kind of deal with

173

Flash Bill Danton and his crew, letting them use trails across Shoestring when they rustled cattle from the settlers. He convinced me he had a damn good reason for doing that and I went along with him. But I've found out since that he lied, made a fool of me. That there could be a lot more than a few widelooped steers involved.'

Jimmy said nothing and Deke let him think about it as he poked aimlessly at the fire.

'Why you want to know anythin' if you're not still a Ranger, Deke?'

'Guess I've been enforcing the law for so long it comes as second nature now. Can't bear to see it broken. But Durango took care of me for a lot of years in the Rangers and I can't stand by and see him walk into trouble when I reckon I can help him out.'

Taggart nodded, but he was in a quandary: mostly afraid of Jno and the others, and certainly Durango Spain himself, but recalling how Deke had stood up for him with Jno and beat the bully for the first time that Taggart knew of.

'I know where they hold some rustled cows, couple of canyons, not far from here, matter of fact. One's on Shoestring, the other just across the river in the Territory, near Cockrel Falls.'

Cutler nodded.

'Well, that's handy to know, Jimmy, and a week ago I'd've been really interested, but since then I've talked with Captain Bannister at Fort Montague – which I'd be obliged if you didn't mention to anyone. Now I'd be more interested in, say, a cave, or a hidden clearing in a thickly wooded area that was hard to get to, but where someone could hide a few wagons – or even a big pile of goods.'

He saw the tightening of Jimmy's eyes and mouth in the flicker of the flames and threw some more wood on the fire. Jimmy looked away, then turned back suddenly, as if reaching a decision.

'There is a place I saw – and there's somethin' there, a big pile of somethin' covered with tarps. Looks like a lot of boxes. I know there's dynamite in some but I ain't sure about the others. I only...'

Deke Cutler leaned forward eagerly.

Then a rifle crashed somewhere out there in the darkness and Jimmy Taggart grunted as the bullet took him and flung him back out of the firelight, a loosely tumbling shadow to add to the other shadows.

CHAPTER 12

NIGHT KILLER

Deke Cutler threw himself backwards out of the circle of light as another bullet slammed into the camp, scattering the fire in an explosion of embers and burning twigs.

Deke's gun was in his hand as he rolled on to his belly, triggering twice. He had caught a glimpse of something bright up there in the timber behind the rocks: it could have been part of the muzzle flash of the killer's rifle seen through bushes. He didn't know if Jimmy was alive or dead but this was no time to go look.

A bullet whined off the rocks up there in the darkness and when the bushwhacker fired next, it was from way over on the left. Deke figured he would shoot and shift position immediately. Ducking another bullet, he waited, and a few moments later a short volley raked the blackness where he lay. Dirt erupted around his body, stung his face with gravel, but he stayed put. Tensed like a coiled

176

spring, he waited until he saw the next muzzle flash – still moving left, which was what he wanted to know.

Immediately he frog-jumped right and hit the dirt with arms and legs spread, flattening his body. Two bullets zipped into the ground and then there was silence and he knew the man would be reloading. Marking the last position, he hastily thumbed two cartridges into the Colt's cylinder, replacing the two he had fired, then rolled swiftly away from the campsite. He fell with a grunt of surprise into an eroded channel coming down from the freshwater spring that they used for the camp. It was wide enough to take his body. There was only a bare trickle but he cursed as he felt the wetness soak through his trousers. Trying to move carefully, he was just in the process of reaching for the far side of the channel when a surge of cold water hit him as if someone had thrown a bucketful at him. It soaked him and reached down his shirtfront, up his neck and along his jaw. He gasped with its chill and started to pull himself up on to the low bank.

Then he paused. The water had dropped to a trickle again. Now what the hell kind of a spring was it that surged up in a minor flood – then dropped back to the usual trickle?

No! Not the spring itself but something that blocked the flow of the trickle briefly, gave it time to build up a little, so that when the obstruction was removed, a couple of gallons were released down the course of the channel....

He smiled to himself.

'Mister, you rolled into that channel, didn't you, moving left as you were. Lay there long enough to stuff some shells into the rifle, figuring it would give you a little protection, water building up against you, then pulled yourself out – *still going left!*'

Well, that last was only a hope, really, but it was logical and Cutler didn't give it any more thought. He slid on to the channel's right bank – the left one for Jno – and moved upwards slowly. The rifle crashed but while he didn't see the stab of the muzzle flash, he saw its brief illumination lighting up the area allowing him to recognize the big man hunched over the weapon, raking the camp once more.

'Save your ammo, Jno!' Deke said. The big man gasped and almost fell in his hurry to swing around towards the voice, rifle lever working.

Deke triggered three fast shots, the would-be killer cried out and there was a sliding sound. The rifle came skittering down the slope first, followed by Jno's tumbling body. Deke rolled out of the way and Jno hung up on a rock, hands trailing into the spring-water in the shallow channel.

Deke grabbed the man's shirt collar and dragged him into camp, dumped him near the remains of the fire and kicked together some of the still burning sticks and embers. As it flared enough to see, he saw that Jno was finished, blood dribbling from his mouth, gut-shot and lung-shot. Cutler moved around carefully, looking for Jimmy Taggart.

He found the kid huddled behind a rock, face twisted in pain, one arm dangling, his shoulder shattered by the bullet. Deke got him back into the light, ripped the necker-chief off the dying Jno and bound up Jimmy's wound. He gave the kid some water. Jimmy coughed, spluttered, drank some more slowly, looking at the bloody man opposite.

'Mighta knowed ... Jno'd stick around ... aimin' to get you, Deke. He don't like bein' beat, only beatin'-up on someone else.'

Cutler merely nodded: he knew Jno had had plenty of time to ride back to Shoe-string and then come back again to pick them both off. Thing was, did he do it of his own accord? Or was he obeying orders?

Deke moved to Jno but there was little he could do for the man. He checked his pockets, found more money than he expected, including a gold fifty-dollar piece. He brewed coffee for himself and Jimmy Taggart as they listened to Jno slowly dying. Jimmy was very white, couldn't take his eyes off the man who had tried to kill him.

'What we gonna do, Deke?'

'I'll strap up your arm. Then we'll go back to the ranch and get you into town to see a sawbones.'

'Reckon it'll be ... safe to go back to Shoestring?' Jimmy looked away quickly, as if embarrassed.

'What d'you mean, "safe", Jim?'

'Well, if Jno did ride back to the ranch, then come back here... He shot at me first, Deke! I've just figured... Maybe someone told him to – kill us – both...'

'Could be. We'll be safe enough going back to Shoestring. But there's something I want you to do for me first, Jim.'

Taggart swallowed and then nodded.

'I know. Tell you where I found that cache of dynamite and whatever else was there.'

Cutler nodded, waiting.

'It happened when I was lookin' for mustangs. I found some tracks, but I knew they wasn't just hosses, looked like some mules were with 'em. Someone'd tried to wipe out the sign and I reckoned that was queer. There was four, five mules and the tracks were deep, so they were carryin' heavy loads.' He paused and grimaced, holding his wounded shoulder gently. 'They led me to that clearin'. It was a helluva job gettin' in there. I found some boxes marked "dynamite", and started to look at the rest, but I thought I heard somethin', like a horse comin', and – well, I was plenty jumpy, Deke, by that time – so I run. Ain't been back since.'

'But you could find it again?'

'I ... could tell you how to find it. I got no hankerin' to go back.'

'That's all I want, Jim.'

Taggart studied Deke's face in the firelight, seeing all the planes and hollows highlighted and shadowed in turn. Cutler looked mighty tough, he thought.

Jimmy remained silent and frowning, impatient, Deke said:

'Kid...?'

Jimmy stirred.

'Yeah, sure. I'll explain on the way back to

181

the ranch. OK?'

Durango listened to Cutler's story in silence while Karen worked gently on Jimmy's shoulder. Spain had poured a couple of big glasses of whiskey into him and he was out to it now, only crying out or groaning when something that Karen did hurt and the pain reached through his oblivion.

'There's a lot of splintered bone,' Karen said anxiously, looking at her husband. 'I'm afraid to dig too deep in case I set it bleeding again. He needs a proper doctor.'

Spain frowned.

'Can't you fix him?' He sounded annoyed and looked angry when she shook her head.

'This is beyond my talents, Durango. That bullet's shattered the bone. He might even have to have the arm amputated.'

'Hell almighty! What the blazes got into Jno?' He glared at Deke suddenly. 'Likely it was you beatin'-up on him, Deke! He sure ain't used to anyone besting him.'

'Why did he bother riding back here first then?' Cutler countered slowly, his gaze holding to Spain's cold eyes. 'If he was riled, all he had to do was hang around and pick us off.'

Durango nodded.

'Yeah, well, he did ride in here. But he

didn't show up for supper and I thought he'd just turned in early after the fight with you.'

Karen was still looking at him, still frowning. Deke shrugged.

'Well, for whatever reason, he was aiming to kill us both. Karen, if you take Jimmy into town, you'd better tell the sheriff about Jno.'

'No need for that,' Durango said quickly. 'I don't want that damn sheriff out here wasting my time asking questions. You go in with Karen and take Jno's body and make your statement, Deke. And make it fast. We're short-handed now. Ringo's still not riding too well yet.'

Deke nodded, appearing to be satisfied.

'So you want me to ride into town with Karen and Jimmy?'

'Don't *want* you to, but it'll be simplest, I guess.'

A buckboard was prepared and Cutler changed his mare for the rested grey and collected an extra box of shells from Spain, who handed them over deadpan.

'Expecting a war?'

'I never know what to expect since I came here, Durango, and that's a fact.'

Spain watched them ride out, Karen driving, Jimmy in the back of the buckboard

183

with Jno's tarp-wrapped corpse. Cutler rode his big grey alongside. Spain knew he could convince the sheriff in Wichita Falls that Jno had acted out of spite and revenge if he had to, so he wasn't worried on that account.

But Deke was still a problem. For some reason he made Spain edgy. Durango was sure his story about dying from cancer had brought Deke around so there would be little or no trouble. But after he went with that Samburu and Dutch Pete fought the bear – well, something else must have happened while he was out there.

Since he had returned, he had been cool to Spain and seemed ready for a fight, almost. What the hell, it could be he had no idea and it riled the hell out of him.

To make sure things went smoothly, he *had* to be in control along the Red River. If he wasn't, there was every chance that Flash Danton and his hardcases would kill him, take over and run amok, with the help from the Indian alliance.

Well, if the sheriff delayed Deke long enough in town – and he was a finicky old bastard – with any luck the whole deal would be finished, signed, sealed and delivered, by the time Cutler got back.

And by then it would be too late.

Way, way too late.

Well clear of the ranch, the sun still low enough to make them squint, Cutler tied the grey on to the tailgate and settled in the seat beside Karen at the reins.

They drove a short distance, then she turned to him, looking worried.

'Deke,' she said quietly, 'Jno did come back to the ranch as Durango said – and I saw Durango give him some money.' She sounded reluctant to part with the information.

Deke fumbled in his pocket and brought out the fifty-dollar gold piece. 'Found this in Jno's pocket.'

He heard her suck in a sharp breath.

'I didn't see how much,' she almost whispered, 'but – but whatever it was glinted quite ... brightly.'

Deke nodded. 'Yeah. Looks like Jno was paid to hit our camp.'

'Oh, Deke! I feel rotten talking about Durango like this but, well, I'm sure he's involved in something. Not just something on the edge of the law, but something quite big.' He waited and she took another deep breath and added: 'He's had Hal Tripp and Ringo and a couple of others getting ready for a long ride. Or if not a long one, one that'll keep them away from the ranch for a while. I asked him and he just snapped at me, said they were going after mavericks and he didn't know how long it would take.' She turned to study his face. 'But we've got more mavericks than we can handle already. There just isn't enough graze for any more.'

'Stop the buckboard, Karen.' He was climbing down in the dust cloud the vehicle had raised before it slid to a complete stop. 'There's something brewing – and it's coming to a head. Can you get a message to Lieutenant Craig at Fort Montague? A short wire'll do: say "Cockrel Falls, NNW three miles. Going in." And sign my name.'

Her eyes were wide.

'Those falls are in the Indian Territory!'

Deke was in the grey's saddle now and he nodded curtly. 'It's mighty important, Karen! If I'm right, it'll affect everyone along the Red River.'

'And if you're wrong?'

'Then I'll ride out and sign over my share in Shoestring to Durango.

'This *thing* you suspect – does it involve Durango?' she asked, a tremor in her voice.

'Very much so, Karen. Very much so! *Adios!*'

He spun the grey and rowelled away towards the foothills. She stared after him, unmoving, watching him swing down to the river trail that skirted the rise.

Deke didn't look back, concentrating on riding hard. She stood in the seat and called his name once, but he didn't hear. Then Jimmy Taggart in the back moaned and started to thrash a little. Biting her lip, she sat down, whipped up the team and raised a long dust cloud on the road into town.

CHAPTER 13

ONCE A RANGER

Finding the patch of heavy timber where Jimmy Taggart said the cache of boxes was took some doing. Deke located the particular mountain, and the sound of falling water drew him to the Cockrel Falls. He approached on the high trail that overlooked the ribbon falls as they plunged in twin strips of lacy water a hundred feet into a pool. Dark lines around the pool's edges showed how much the level had gone down without rain.

Deke's gaze was restless, probing the hollows and shadows amongst the rocks. About half-way up, he saw Ringo, settled in the midst of some boulders that clung to the steep side of the slope, watching the lower trail.

Cutler dismounted, leaving the grey inside the line of trees. He left his hat and spurs behind, slid over the edge, spray wetting him, and began to climb down. Twice he

188

slipped, boots skidding across wet rocks, but he didn't dislodge anything and Ringo didn't look up: he even set his rifle to one side and began to make a cigarette. Deke could hear him humming some range ditty.

It all helped to cover Deke's approach and when he was about eight feet above Ringo, trying to figure out where to place his boots next, the projecting rock he was standing on one-footed, gave way. It pulled out of the damp soil with a slight sucking sound that made Ringo start and look up, dropping his makings. And then Deke was hurtling down to land almost on top of the man.

He jarred down with a grunt and instinctively grabbed at something for support. The something was Ringo, and the hardcase swore, shoved him away and dived for his rifle. Deke got his balance fast enough to pluck a handful of mud from the steep earthen wall and he flung it savagely. It took Ringo in the face and the man staggered into a boulder. The rifle fell and Deke heard it splash into the pool, then Ringo was lifting his hands, half-crouched.

'Easy! I – I ain't in any shape to fight you, Cutler!'

The man winced and pressed an elbow into his left side. Deke guessed this was where he had been wounded. And while his gaze was momentarily distracted to that part of Ringo's body, the man's right hand flew up to the back of his neck and Deke's mind screamed a warning: the blacksmith had said Ringo favoured knives....

Deke dived left and the blade flashed past his face, thunked into the wet earth. Ringo swore and went for his six-gun but Deke didn't want gunfire now. He ripped the knife free and lunged at Ringo. The man's scream as the knife pierced his heart was muffled by Deke's free hand clamping across his mouth. Deke let him fall, and he tumbled down to crash on the rocks at the edge of the pool.

Breathing hard, Deke climbed the rest of the way down and started to drag Ringo's body out of sight. Then he thought of Lieutenant Craig and his soldiers and propped the dead man up amongst the rocks, using several stones and a dead branch to support the man's right arm. He folded back all the fingers except one, pointing the way to the high trail, and hoped the young Lieutenant would understand.

The climb back to the grey left him breathless. He drank from the canteen as he looked for the landmark of the lightning-struck shagbark hickory tree. It was an old one, nearing the hundred feet maximum height, and it was split almost a third of the way down, one splintered arm hung up in the branches of neighbouring trees. It made a sizeable landmark even from a couple of miles away.

Due north for a mile, swing west and drop downslope into a thick, dark stand of cedar... Those had been Jimmy Taggart's instructions and Cutler followed them to the letter, riding the grey with his rifle held at the ready, using knee pressures to guide the horse. When he came to the brush that blocked further advance, he dismounted. As he stood beside the sweating horse, rubbing its neck idly, listening to the buzz and hum of insects and a distant swish of a breeze high up in the branches of the cedars, he heard a crackling sound like twigs breaking. Then there came the faint whinny of a horse and he quickly clamped a hand over the grey's muzzle.

The sounds came from hard left and he turned that way, hearing them more clearly. He looped the grey's reins over a bush, started forward, placing his boots carefully so as to avoid dead twigs and leaves.

Sweat drenched him in here. Once he felt a slight breeze touch his damp skin and he began to walk in that direction. Then, he heard men's voices, not far off...

Deke tightened his grip on his rifle, crouched lower, using the Winchester's muzzle to push aside branches to ease his passage. And then he jumped at the sudden braying of a mule, away on his right, stumbling into a bush. As it shook some of the deader branches snapped. He fell to his knees in the open, saw the clearing, stacked boxes and crates, discarded tarps lying on the ground. Men worked at sorting and transferring boxes to a waiting string of mules.

Then he was seen, and someone yelled. Boxes were dropped as the men immediately reached for their guns.

The old Ranger training took over and Deke Cutler dived for the ground, shooting in the general direction of the men, not caring whether he hit anyone or anything, just as long as they scattered. They did, yelling, and some men started shooting back right away, bullets going wild.

Deke skidded under a bush, levered in a fresh shell, fired, rolled away, forced his way back into deeper shadow. He nailed his first outlaw with the next shot, picking the man off as he ran for the cover of a pile of long, narrow boxes. The man went down all flailing arms and legs, knocking one of his companions off his feet. Deke shot him, too, but he didn't think it was fatal. And then a volley of concentrated fire raked the brush and twigs rained down on his shoulders, dirt erupted into his face. He got his feet under him and lunged to his right, then instantly swung back and dived headlong. More bullets ripped through the brush but over to his left. He slid quickly under branches and emptied the rifle at the still running men. He saw a man's leg kick out to one side, its owner tumbling, trying to crawl into cover. He looked like a man he had seen with Flash Bill Danton. Then he saw Danton himself, rising with a shotgun at his shoulder.

Deke rolled frantically, hurling himself wildly aside. The brush above him was torn apart, buckshot cleaving branches and leaves. They rained down on him in a swarming cloud, the bush ripping apart. The second barrel discharged with a brief thunder and more buckshot rattled mighty close above his head, several balls stinging his back, one burning his leg. It twitched and he grabbed at it, feeling a little blood trickling already.

He lunged up and started to run for the protection of a tree when a man loomed up to one side, yelling, *'Deke!'* Cutler spun around, and a rifle butt crashed into his head.

Just before the world exploded in a sheet of flame, Deke recognized Durango Spain.

'How the hell did he find this place, that's what I want to know – and I mean now, Durango!'

Flash Bill Danton's distinctive voice hammered through the thumping roar in Deke's head and he opened his eyes slightly, peering through interlaced lashes. They had dragged him nearer the stash of boxes and crates. Now he could read stencilled names on some: DYNAMITE on the slab-sided boxes with the hinged lids, and on the long, narrow boxes with the bracing-timbers nailed a foot in from each end, US ARMY RIFLES. Some square boxes just on the edge of his vision he recognized as those made to carry ammunition.

So Bannister was right, he thought, remembering the captain at Fort Montague telling him he suspected a load of stolen arms had been taken across the Red River to be sold for an Indian uprising. Deke only realized he had spoken aloud when Danton and Spain snapped their heads around towards him. He started to sit up, remembering in time not to appear too fit. He wasn't yet tied up – which could mean he was marked for death, though

Durango could easily have killed him instead of knocking him out. He lifted a shaking hand to the goose-egg sized knot above his right eye.

'What the hell hit me?'

'I did,' Spain snapped. 'I should've shot you!'

'Yeah, you should've,' growled Danton, kicking Deke in the side roughly. 'How'd you find this place?'

Deke swung his eyes towards Spain and smiled devilishly.

'Why, Durango showed me a sketch map when he was figuring on cutting me in on the deal.'

The more dissension and suspicion he could foster the better, he figured.

Spain's eyes flew wide in real alarm.

'You goddamn liar!' he shouted looking swiftly at Danton. 'It's not true, Bill! He's just trying to make trouble!'

'Is that right?' Danton gritted. 'You been showin' him a soft spot all along, Durango! I wanted him dead soon as he arrived, but you talked me around, sayin' you could handle him. Well, you ain't done it! Soon as you found that Springfield cartridge on him, you shoulda killed him! But I'll take care of that, right now!'

Danton's six-gun blurred out of leather but Spain jumped forward, quickly pushed his hand down.

'Wait! For Chris'sakes, *wait!* We *have* to know how he got here, who else he told. Judas, I figured he'd be held up in Wichita Falls with that damn sheriff over Jno's shooting and–'

'He likely got your wife to wire the goddamn soldiers!' Danton cut in and kicked Deke viciously, making him draw his knees swiftly up to his chest, rolling from side to side, moaning in pain. 'Huh? That right, you son of a bitch?'

Spain leaned down over him, twisted his fingers in Deke's hair, lifted his head and slammed it down on the ground.

'*Did* you talk her round? I know you could do it, because she still cares for you! She never stops talking about you! Wept herself dry when we heard you were dead. Christ, I had to try and hold on to her somehow, but it took money to buy the things she was accustomed to. You think I'd deal with scum like Danton otherwise?'

Spain turned irritably as Danton hit him roughly on the shoulder. The outlaw bared his teeth.

'Did you say "scum" like me?'

Spain frowned, still angry.

'Hell, I dunno. I was just talking. But if it wasn't for Cutler I would never've had anything to do with you – except to shoot you on sight.'

Danton nodded amiably.

'Figured you felt that way. Well, it's mutual, Durango, old hoss, dead – mutual!'

And he fired point blank into Spain, the bullet knocking Durango back almost six feet before he collapsed in a heap. Then Danton screamed as Deke drew Ringo's knife from the top of his riding-boot where he had hidden it, and drove it into Danton's leg, the only part of him he could reach. Flash Bill howled and danced away, his gun blasting wildly into the ground. He couldn't keep his balance and Deke threw himself at Spain, rolling towards him, hoping to grab his six-gun. The man was too far away: he would never make it. But Spain wasn't yet dead and he threw his Colt towards Deke.

Cutler scooped it up, spun on to his side and drove two bullets into Flash Bill Danton as the man rose to one knee, face screwed up in pain from his deeply slashed leg. Deke's bullets wiped that and every other expression from his features and Danton slammed over backwards, dead.

The other men started shooting now and Deke felt the tug of lead against his right sleeve. He rolled towards the nearest pile of boxes. The outlaws were yelling and running, not sure how many intruders there were or what was happening.

Cutler wasn't too sure himself, his head spinning.

Then Hal Tripp recognized Deke and started firing wildly. The men had made their way to some rocks, moving away from the cache of weapons and dynamite so there would be no risk of stray bullets setting off a charge. Deke made a zigzagging run to where the pile of boxes were and dived behind them. The outlaws started shooting instinctively.

'Stop! Stop, for Chris'sakes!,' yelled Tripp. 'There's enough dynamite there to blow down half the mountain!' Tripp wasn't taking any chances that a bullet just might set off the dynamite though it would need to be very old and unstable for that to happen. Deke used the man's panic to his own advantage. Safely behind the first row of stacked boxes, he thumbed fresh loads from his bullet belt. He spun around, shooting between two boxes. A man yelled but no bullets answered Deke's shots. He crouched down, pulled one of the dynamite boxes towards him and lifted the hinged lid. There were sticks of dynamite, fuse lengths and a waxed cardboard cylinder with detonator caps packed in cotton wool inside.

Taking time to check where the others were, he pushed a detonator into the end of a stick of dynamite, crimped the fuse on to the copper nipple with his teeth, then lit a cigarillo he had found earlier in the pocket of the shirt he had borrowed from Spain. He touched the glowing end to the fuse, waited for it to splutter and hurled it in the general direction of the rocks.

Two men were creeping slowly towards his hiding place, belly down, obviously hoping to surprise him. One saw the trail of smoke arcing down towards them and screamed a warning, jumping up to run back towards the rocks. He was too late – as was his companion. The dynamite exploded with gouting fire and fountains of earth – and a couple of human limbs mixed in. It had a mighty sobering effect on the others still cowering amongst the boulders. Deke prepared another stick and hurled it towards them. It fell short but the explosion brought frightened swearing and dire threats.

Then he heard the crunch of stones, like a

boot turning on gravel. Deke spun, and between the boxes, saw a man with a rifle only yards away. The man went to ground, panicked when he saw that Deke had spotted him, and fired one-handed. The bullet chewed a large splinter out of the corner of a box of dynamite but there was no explosion. The outlaw actually laughed in relief, jumped to his feet and, with a savage Rebel yell, charged in on Deke's hiding-place, working lever and trigger on his rifle. Deke rolled clear, flopped on to his belly and fired at the wild man. The outlaw staggered and swung his gun towards Deke but Cutler brought him down with another bullet.

At the same time he saw Tripp and three others running towards him. They were shooting because he was yards away from the dynamite now, but Deke took a flying dive, scooped up another stick he had prepared, jammed the end against the burning cigarillo he had clamped between his teeth and hurled it at the advancing men.

They turned to run and the dynamite exploded over their heads, the concussion knocking them flat. They lay stunned, but Hal Tripp lurched up, wild-eyed, gun in hand. Deke's last bullet sent his body somersaulting over a boulder. Then he saw more men coming out of the rocks. He groaned – his six-gun was empty and there were no more sticks of dynamite prepared. The men had realized his predicament and let out a roar as they ran in, shooting. Even as he fumbled at his bullet belt, Deke knew it was way too late.

Then there was a series of hoarse cries near the tree-line and Deke, starting to hunt cover, jerked around. Soldiers on foot were charging in, rifles spitting flame, the heavy balls whistling before knocking over some of the outlaws, felling them like a row of skittles. Lieutenant Craig was in the lead, his pistol barking. The soldiers swept around in a tight arc, trapping those outlaws still standing. They quickly threw down their guns, lifting their hands high, coughing in the thick pall of gunsmoke.

Lieutenant Craig, face sweating, hurried across to Deke.

'You're early,' Deke panted.

'Bit of luck. Ran into Mrs Spain on the way into town and I – er – appreciated your somewhat macabre signpost back at the falls, pointing the way here. Saved a lot of time.'

'Bannister was right the other day when he said Durango and Danton were in the gun-running business.' There was dejection and sadness in Deke's voice.

'Well – not quite. *Danton* was definitely supplying guns to this new alliance of the Indian tribes, but Durango Spain...' His voice trailed off and Deke frowned, looking towards Spain where a corpsman was working over him.

'What about Durango?' he asked hoarsely.

'Let's see how badly he's hurt.'

Cutler followed the officer to where Spain lay, bloody rags covering the chest wound. Craig looked quizzically at the corpsman who shook his head slowly. Spain reached up a hand, eyes pain-filled and glazing.

'F-fooled you,' he gasped.

Deke turned to Craig.

'What's he mean?'

The lieutenant saw that Spain wouldn't be doing much talking and explained succinctly:

'Captain Bannister briefed me before we set out. When Spain captured Danton down on the Rio, Flash knew Durango was about to be married and was low on funds. He bribed Spain to let him go, substituted another body so Spain could claim the bounty.' He looked sharply at Cutler. 'Did you know Danton had saved Spain's life during the war – twice?'

Deke hadn't known that. Now he felt his

body tingle, realizing Spain hadn't been as corrupt as everyone thought. Weak, sure, on the eve of his marriage, and broke but... A debt like he owed Danton would be the one thing that would make him bend the law, deviate from his own strict code. Still...

'Not acceptable, though, Craig,' Deke said tightly and the lieutenant nodded.

'Danton had been wanted for a long time because his supplying the rebels with arms had caused a big rift, politically, between the United States and Mexico. The Rangers somehow got wind of the deal and Spain was hauled up to Headquarters. No excuses, they said, and told Spain he was facing dishonourable dismissal and jail. Then a federal marshal turned up and offered him a deal.

'They believed Danton was heading north to back an Indian uprising in the Territory. The US marshals were very interested but didn't have anyone to send in undercover. So they offered Spain an honourable discharge from the Rangers, with pension. He was to work his ranch on the Red River where Danton had been seen, and spread the word he was ready for more easy money. He would allow Danton to use Shoestring to take rustled herds into the Territory, and once Danton trusted Spain, the Rangers figured he'd be cut in on the arms deal. Spain could hardly refuse. Then you turned up, months ahead of schedule and Durango had to try and keep you from getting involved...'

Deke stared down at Durango whose eyes were fluttering as he tried to hold on a little longer.

'You kept me at arm's length, so I wouldn't butt in and spoil your set-up,' he said quietly, 'letting me think you'd turned outlaw just for a few fast bucks...'

'Didn't want you getting all hotheaded. I couldn't tell you about it, Deke. Thought the cancer story would hold you. Anyway, I figured if anything happened to me you'd be there for Karen to fall back on.'

Deke was on one knee now, holding Spain's limp right hand.

'You're a damn good pard, Durango! But what about Jno trying to kill Jimmy and me?'

'His idea. He was s'posed to drive off the mustangs ... keep you busy ... rounding 'em up ... while Danton showed me where the ... guns were hidden.'

Deke smiled crookedly.

'Once a Ranger, eh?'

Spain shuddered, and there was a brief, sudden strength in his grip. He coughed blood.

'Deke ... not much time ... you know ... how I want to be ... buried. Tell Karen I ... lo–' He sighed, went limp, breathed one last ragged gasp.

'I'll look after her, Durango,' Deke said quietly.

'I'm sorry, Deke,' Craig said. 'With your past record we were afraid you'd buy in at the wrong time. Spain had gone to a lot of trouble to set it up, playing the corrupt rancher. If you believed it, we knew Danton would, too.'

Deke nodded: he savvied all that.

'But where do Dutch Pete and Sam fit in? *If* they do...'

Craig smiled thinly.

'The guns. They were stolen from a ship at Vera Cruz on their way to the US Army, via Mexico. Politics again. The Army was mighty short of weapons and these were cheap and reliable, a new kind of repeater, but made in South Africa by a Dutch arms company with a lot of very quiet American money behind it. There'd be big trouble if the local arms manufacturers knew about it. The South Africans sent us van Rensberg, their top investigator, who also happened to be actually crazy for danger. They set him up on a ranch, and his job was to scout the

Territory looking for the guns. A damn good cover, really, an eccentric hunter like that, free to wander wherever he liked. He was getting very close to locating the guns. In fact it was the toss of a coin whether he or Spain would find the guns first. We think van Rensburg was about to reveal to you that he'd found the guns when that bear arrived at the wrong time. He still believed Spain was in it with Danton. We were waiting, as you know, ready to move on Pete's word.'

Deke smiled.

'Crazy, I'd call him, not eccentric! But game as they come!'

Craig shrugged, smiling.

'By the way, Mrs Spain said she'll wait for you in the hotel lobby in Wichita Falls.'

Cutler nodded soberly, looking down at Spain.

'Got to bury Durango first. He wants it to be on high ground, overlooking a river. You know a place?'

'I think so. But what then, Deke?'

'Guess I'll ride into Wichita Falls.'

'To see Dutch Pete or ... Mrs Spain?'

Deke smiled faintly.

'Both. Karen'll need to be told about Durango, then...' He shrugged. 'I guess we'll work something out.'

The publishers hope that this book has given you enjoyable reading. Large Print Books are especially designed to be as easy to see and hold as possible. If you wish a complete list of our books please ask at your local library or write directly to:

Dales Large Print Books
Magna House, Long Preston,
Skipton, North Yorkshire.
BD23 4ND

This Large Print Book, for people
who cannot read normal print,
is published under the auspices of

THE ULVERSCROFT FOUNDATION